FAREWELL KISS

Special Indian Edition

BY TRISTIANA KINK
& RIYA KAPOOR

Farewell Kiss: Special Indian Edition

By Tristiana Kink and Riya Kapoor

© 2020 Tristiana Kink and Riya Kapoor
First edition

All rights reserved. This book or parts thereof may not be reproduced in any form, stored in any retrieval system, or transmitted in any form by any means - electronic, mechanical, photocopy, recording, or otherwise - without prior written permission of the publisher, except as provided by United States of America copyright law.

Any similarity to real people, places or actions is purely coincidental.

CONTENTS

Chapter 1	1
Chapter 2	14
Chapter 3	26
Chapter 4	30
Chapter 5	38
Chapter 6	48
Chapter 7	57
Chapter 8	63
Chapter 9	71
Chapter 10	76
Chapter 11	88

Chapter 1

"I can't live like this anymore, please don't cry after me, I hate myself for doing all the bad things to you and I hope one day you will forgive me. You will be happier when I am gone so I don't screw anything else… I'm so sorry, goodbye forever. God and you please forgive me. Rakesh."

Karishma was reading this over and over, crumpling the paper of the smushed letter. She was sitting on the big wooden bed in an old apartment building that was far away from the Mumbai's center. He was in the bathroom, getting ready for their farewell sex. That was all she managed to get from him - she felt like it was the last piece of food from the master's hand, thrown to his faithful but unloved dog.

Over the past months she had been coming here often, but today was the last one time - the last time she would see Rakesh, she would to be able to touch him, to kiss him passionately as she always did, and the last time they would have sex in their secret spot. She knew it was a goodbye. He told her many times that their clandestine relationship must end. That his wife and children were too precious for him to lose over her.

"So what was that between us?" Karishma thought to herself, "Just a fling?"

She knew she would miss the amazing sex, the electric feel of their bodies touching, the way they kissed, the way she felt they can be together forever. But today she was ready, very ready to give up on all of that.

She looked at the letter again and smiled as she reminisced about all the first day they had met and how they found themselves in this peculiar situation.

***

It was an exceptionally hot and muggy day at the end of the monsoon season. Karishma arrived at the hospital a little late. She rushed to change into her nurse's uniform and skipped past a few routines "hi" and "hellos" in the hospital corridor. She ran into her managing doctor in the hallway while looking at a patient's chart.

"Hello Doctor, sorry I am late, the traffic was horrible." she lied.

"Karishma, you know you can't be late. This is a hospital, not a family ran restaurant." Doctor Patwari gave her a sour but still teasing smile.

Doctor Patwari was the chief of staff for the Critical Care unit at the Hospital bit east from Malabar Hill. He was starting to lose a bit of hair, but it somehow made him more masculine. He was a decent boss most of the time, but Karishma always felt uncomfortable around him as he would often stare at her breasts like he wanted to grab them any minute. This always confused her - she was just an average girl and didn't understand why Doctor Patwari was teasing her. Karishma always thought she was the kind of woman that people described as sweet and nice rather than sexy or hot. She stood about 5'3 with shoulder-length black hair and a few freckles. Some people had gone far enough to call the freckles cute, but she thought they looked like stains of coffee on her face.

She wouldn't call herself ugly, but certainly she knew she wasn't a beauty turning men's heads - just an average girl from the neighborhood. Long days at the hospital on her feet kept her from getting out of shape but she still wished she had time for the gym. Maybe then someone other than perverted Doctor Patwari would be glancing at her.

She had never been the lucky one with love. It's so hard to find someone special when she spends so much time at the hospital. Her family tried to set her up for some dates, but she was never up to this. She even tried dating websites and then meeting guys in public places like coffee shops, but all the guys she met just wanted to get laid. The only exception was Varun. She thought he could have been different than other guys and for some time the things went so well between them, until they ran out of luck and just like with all the other ones it went bad. That didn't stop Karishma from thinking about Varun often. Sometimes she would lose track of time and spend hours looking at his old messages and very few photos they had together. That was the reason why she was late today, she fell into that vast rabbit hole of digging into memories again.

"We have a new patient that I want you to take care of," Doctor Patwari brought her back to her senses.

"Ok, sir," Karishma replied evenly.

"His name is Rakesh Anand. He was brought in this morning from the emergency ward. He had a nasty motorbike accident," Doctor Patwari explained, "Currently, he is stable but sedated. He has a fractured leg and a dislocated elbow. He is on bed rest for at least a week as we saw some inconsistencies in his vital signs. You would be taking care of him until he is released. And Mr. Anand is an important patient, so please make sure he gets the first-class care."

"Alright Doctor. In which room is he?" Karishma asked, but the doctor was staring at her breasts again.

"Which room doctor?" she asked out louder, blushing all over her face.

"Ah, Room 23B," Doctor replied nervously, but Karishma saw the little smirk of satisfaction on his face that made her even more embarrassed. She started walking towards the room 23B with her back towards the Doctor, and she could feel his creepy eyes on her ass.

She opened the door to the room 23B and looked at an unconscious man in a hospital bed. Immediately she felt a warmth spreading across her body. The patient was a tall, probably around 6'2 handsome man, looking more like Lord Shiva than a real person. He was well built, with fair skin tone, had a beautiful nose and lips that were carved for kissing. He was in his mid-forties but looked fit like an athlete. Her heart raced as she looked at him.

Karishma prided herself on always being professional… Well, almost always, but something struck her about this new patient. She hadn't been that taken with a patient since Varun. But even with Varun it wasn't quite like this, it took her a few good days to feel the same warmth she was feeling right now. Her mind started racing as she looked upon Mr. Anand.

"How can a man be so stunningly beautiful, but so manly at the same time?" she asked herself rhetorically. Her fantasy flashed quickly to anger. "He is probably just like all the other guys. So what if he is gorgeous… but maybe… maybe he could be different." Her conflicting thoughts were interrupted as the door popped open.

"He's a cutie pie, isn't he?" Karishma heard a voice from behind that snapped her back to reality.

It was Vinita, another nurse in the ward. Vinita was a typical beauty, having every aspect of a top Bollywood star; smooth skin, tall, with the long silky hair and pearly smile. She was skinny but had a sexy booty and big breasts, that Karishma was almost certain that were fake. But for Karishma everything was perfect about Vinita - the first time she saw Vinita, even she lusted after her for a second. She loved looking at her fair skin in a white nurse gown, that was highlighting her perfectly curved body moving like an exotic cat. Of course, Vinita was well aware of her beauty and she came to Mumbai with the idea of becoming the movie star, but in the meantime, she had to work to make her living

"I prepped him this morning," Vinita whispered to her ear while looking at the unconscious man. "He has a huge thingy, yummy" Vinita described Mr. Anand's penis while sticking her tongue out and seductively licking her lips.

"Shut up, Vinita," Karishma blushed.

Vinita always acted like a slut, lusting after doctors, patients, and even female nurses. Karishma thought she was just joking around to keep things exciting during the long shifts. Vinita always made her laugh even if the jokes made Karishma a bit uncomfortable.

The rest of the hospital wasn't as hot on Vinita and some dirty rumors were going around that she was preying on student doctors and even that she slept with Doctor Patwari. "That's impossible, who would want to have sex with Doctor Patwari? Vinita could do so much better. No way." Karishma would think to herself. Not that Doctor Patwari was terrible looking, it's just that he was a creep and Vinita was hot enough to get any man she wanted. Why would she settle for Doctor Patwari?

"I swear Kari that if I get a chance, I will suck his giant cock, even if he is unconscious." Vinita sucked her finger, pretending it was new patient's dick.

"Oh, Vinita, you are so full of crap," Karishma said pretending she was upset, but in reality, she was trying to imagine his penis.

"Why were you late today Kari?" Vinita asked changing the topic.

"Traffic" replied Karishma with overconfidence that even for her sounded fake.

"Pfff! C'mon, I know you good enough not to believe you, you live almost next to hospital! So what was it?" Vinita was always good at catching her lies.

"It's nothing. I just had a date last night," Karishma lied to get Vinita off her back. She didn't feel like explaining that she lost track of time reading old messages from her ex. Vinita burst into laughter. "Whoopee, you little dirty girl. You guys kissed all night and you couldn't get up in the morning, huh?" Vinita was visibly amused, "Even little Karishi needs some charam anand, right girl?"

"Yep, that was it, whatever." Karishma admitted with a sarcastic tone. "I think Doctor Patwari wanted to see you today," she skillfully changed the subject, exhaling with relief.

"Ok, you enjoy your time with our generously gifted Shahid Kapoor and I'll check what this slave master wants from me again," Vinita turned gracefully towards the doors, just like an actress in a movie.

"Who you got today?" Karishma asked quickly before Vinita left.

"Mr. Brendon! That old American fuck got constipation. Again!" Vinita answered in a theatrical whisper and left Karishma alone closing loudly the doors.

Karishma sight and sat in a chair. She idly analyzed Rakesh's chart. "Fractured leg, dislocated elbow, blood results ok, extensive bruising, possible minor concussion. An IV drip of standard anti-inflammatory followed by 500 mg 3x daily. Strong painkillers 4x daily with remark to avoid acetylsalicylic acid, as patient is severely allergic to it. VIP treatment required." The last sentence was bolded and highlighted in red and Karishma found it quite interesting. The VIP treatment was saved for big-name donors to the hospital. Normally, they were very old, wrinkled guys, not good-looking men like Mr. Anand.

When she finished reading and filling her forms, she went to give the daily report to Doctor Patwari. She found him standing at the reception desk waiting for her.

"We have a slight problem. The evening shift nurse had an emergency. I need you to stay and work the evening shift," Doctor Patwari said, "I hope it won't be a problem."

"No Sir, no problem at all" Karishma said as if she had any other option. There was never an option with Doctor Patwari. The ward was his kingdom and he knew it.

"Great! This new patient needs someone to keep a close eye on him and think you are the perfect girl for the job," Patwari explained. " I'm also here for the night shift, so I will come to check on you. Well... I mean on the patient, of course." Doctor Patwari again was looking at her cleavage more than her face. "Get back to our patient. This week he is your main customer, VIP treatment. Anything he wants, you deliver." he said blankly leaving to his office.

Karishma came back to Mr. Anand's room and sat on the chair in front of him. She closed her eyes and trying to imagine how does his voice sounded.

"You know you are not supposed to sleep while on duty, even when you are tired after your bang-bang kiss kiss night. What are you still doing here?" Vinita startled Karishma as she hadn't even heard her coming into the room.

"Damn, girl! You scared me," Karishma could hear her heartbeats. "Navjot had an emergency, so I have to fill in tonight," Karishma answered with a sour voice, but she didn't mind having to stay with her new patient longer. Nurse Navjot was usually assigned to take care of patients in the evenings and nights.

"Yeah! That sucks," Vinita replied.

"But why are you still here?" asked Karishma.

"Hmm, I have some stuff to do," said Vinita while biting her lower lip.

"What stuff?" Karishma sensed some stress in her friend's voice.

"Some work stuff, just some boring nurse stuff" Vinita answered and left the room as quickly as she came in.
"Well, that was strange, even for her" Karishma thought but she really didn't care. She was more curious about her new patient, so she got up to check on Mr. Anand. She took his vitals and checked his temperature when an evil thought crossed her mind.
"What if I just checked if Vinita was right about his gigantic manhood?" she thought, "I could just look quickly under his blanket. He is wearing a gown, so it wouldn't be hard to take a little peek," she tried to convince herself. She caught herself swiftly lowering his blanket to reveal his body wrapped in a hospital gown. Karishma could already tell that Vinita didn't lie this time, Mr. Anand had a significant one. Its glorious shape was distinctly presenting itself through the sheets. Just when she was about to grab his gown and look under it, the nurse inside of her told her to stop. "What am I doing?" she thought, "I have never done this to a patient. I need to clear my mind." She covered him back and went outside to get fresh air.

After wandering around the quiet hospital, Karishma decided to go back to the nurse's room to get some rest. On the way, she heard a muffled sound coming from one of the rooms. There wasn't any patient assigned to that room, it was supposed to be empty. She figured that maybe an older patient got lost trying to find the toilet.

Karishma was about to open the door when she heard a very distinct woman's voice moaning "Oh Yes!" That surely wasn't a lost patient, that was someone having sex in the hospital! Karishma thought of leaving them alone but her curiosity won. She decided to take a little peek, mostly just to see which patients were behaving so inappropriately.

She heard the stories about patients having sex in the hospital, but she never believed them. She always thought that it was one of many perverted stories Vinita is making up to kill time. Vinita was also telling stories about people having sex with dolphins, a man being raped by the gorilla lady in a jungle, and a woman officially marrying her Golden Retriever named Cole somewhere in United States. Karishma laughed at all those silly stories and didn't believe any of them, including the one about people having sex in her Hospital. Vinita was fun to be around because of her silliness and lightness.

Karishma tried to peek through the keyhole but couldn't see much; all she could see were two naked bodies joined together. Even more curious now, she slowly cracked the door open to take a better look. Her heart was beating like crazy. She was equally excited and scared at the chance of being discovered by the couple.

When the pair changed the position, she finally could recognize the faces. It was Doctor Patwari and Vinita. Karishma couldn't believe her eyes, but it was right in front of her. Doctor Patwari was laying on the hospital bed, and Vinita was riding him. And she was riding him hard. Her big ass was bouncing up and down on Doctor Patwari's penis. They were both naked, and Doctor Patwari had his eyes closed while grabbing Vinita's oversized breasts and squeezing them. Vinita looked like a girl trying to ride a rodeo bull, making a slapping sound that filled the room.

"Yes, Patwari, give it to me" Vinita moaned while moving rhythmically on his cock.

Karishma observed the scene in a state of shock. But at the same time seeing Vinita and Doctor Patwari having passionate sex turned her on and she wanted to see more. She looked around, but she knew no one would be coming to this part of the hospital anytime soon. Karishma was safe to stay for a bit longer. She slowly took her fingers and placed them over her pants on her vagina. She gently started rubbing her clit through the fabric and put her other hand on her mouth to not make any kind of noise.

At the same time, Vinita lowered her face to Doctor Patwari's face and they kissed passionately. "I want to have you from behind," Doctor Patwari panted to Vinita. Vinita willingly changed position onto on her knees with hands resting on the bed, ready for doggy style. Doctor Patwari came from behind her and entered his penis inside her vagina with one colossal thrust. He moved it in and out of her with a quickening pace. He held Vinita from her hips and humped her from behind. Vinita was pushing her sun-kissed ass back on his manhood, trying to meet the momentum of the doctor's thumping. Karishma, who was silently watching this steamy sex, was stunned by how horny she was. She could feel her fingers dampened even from over her pants.

"I'm about to cum," gasped the doctor. "Where do you want it?"

"I want it inside me, Doctor" Vinita exhaled lustfully, "Fill me with your cum!" As soon as Vinita said it, Patwari squeezed her hips and pushed his entire length inside of her. From the look on his face, Karishma could tell he was coming. Vinita moaned loudly like she had forgotten where they were. The Doctor shivered with the pleasure of his orgasm; he also seemed to have forgotten where he was.

Karishma quickly realized that she should go back before it was too late. She slid away from the cracked door and headed towards her patient's room. She checked on her patient then sat on the chair, closing her eyes. She needed to wrap her head around everything that had happened today. Maybe she should start giving Vinita's stories more credit, she thought. Still shocked, Karishma found herself at the same time turned on by everything she had seen. She closed her eyes and started to replay the picture of Vinita riding Doctor Patwari. She drifted off to sleep and began to dream.

Karishma found herself in a doggy position with someone pounding her from behind. She could feel the wet dick sliding in and out of her lubed vagina. She turned around to see who was inside of her. It was Doctor Patwari. Karishma realized she was in the body of Vinita. Her big tits bounced to the steady rhythm of the humping. He went faster and faster until she suddenly felt the warm cum shooting inside of her. Karishma shook with a short but intense orgasm. Suddenly, she was back in her own body. The doctor was gone and Karishma saw Vinita walking towards her. Vinita's naked body resembled a renaissance painting. Vinita held Karishma's face in her hands and kissed her. Karishma couldn't move away from her.

"See! I knew you were a slut," Vinita whispered in her ear. Vinita's tongue was penetrating her mouth while her hands headed down south to Karishma's clitoris.

"Excuse me. Hello! Excuse me, nurse!" an unfamiliar voice woke Karishma up from her sleep. She didn't want to leave this dream yet, as Vinita's lips were so soft and warm, but the voice from outside slowly destroyed the dream. She opened her eyes and saw her VIP patient sitting up in his bed, looking at her with curiosity.

"Oh! I am sorry. I must have fallen asleep," Karishma apologized, standing up and trying to fix her uniform and tidy her hair.

"It's totally fine. I just woke up myself," said Mr. Anand with a flirtatious smile. "How long was I out for?"

"About twenty-four hours. You were sedated" Karishma replied while noting his vital signs.
"Wow! Twenty-four hours," said Mr. Anand surprised. "How bad was it? When can I go home?" he asked politely gently smiling at her, and it melted Karishma's heart.

"We worried a bit about your condition, but you are stable now," she looked into his beautiful eyes." We will keep you a bit longer as your vital signs are not satisfactory yet. It wouldn't be longer than a week." she felt like she was sinking in his blue eyes.

"A week?!" Mr. Anand didn't seem happy with this information, "What will I do here?"

"We will take good care of you, Sir," Karishma replied and their eyes met. For a few seconds they just looked into each other's eyes in silence.

"Please don't call me Sir. Call me Rakesh," Mr. Anand broke the silence, "Can I use the bathroom, my dear Karishma?" He read her name from the badge. Karishma swore that this was the softest way to say her name she has ever heard.

"Of course, you can Sir. I mean Rakesh," she blushed saying his name aloud for the first time. "But you have broken leg, so I will serve you with my assistance." Karishma even to herself sounded like she tried a bit too hard.

"I am not used to beautiful ladies to hold my willy when I am peeing. Helping me with the walker should be enough," he looked at her with the playful spark in his eyes.

She felt a quick flash of disappointment as he hobbled into the bathroom. She would have gladly helped him or held anything for him at that moment, but the idea quickly left her head as she pulled her focus back on to her VIP patient.

She helped him to stand up and he made it to the bathroom with the help of a walker. Karishma sat there thinking of what had just happened. His eyes were like some deep ocean that she could drown in. The beautiful blue of his eyes was seductive and secretive at the same time. She wasn't attracted to any patient like this before; she wasn't attracted to anyone like this ever before. Even with Varun, they had some instant chemistry, that later developed into full attraction, but he didn't make her so wildly distracted like this. It was like someone lit a fire in her mind and every time Rakesh moved or spoke it was like throwing wood on top. Rakesh had something in his aura that Karishma found very attractive. But she had to stay professional, after all she was here to take care of her patients and not to get attracted to them. Karishma knew that she was going to have a hard time focusing on her job for the next week.

Chapter 2

Karishma finished her double shift and she was finally released to enjoy a day off. Usually, after a long shift, all she wanted to do was to eat something, relax and not think about the hospital. But not today… Today the hospital, and even more her new patient, kept taking over her thoughts. Every time she closed her eyes she saw Rakesh's face. Maybe it was the lack of sleep or long hours of work, but she couldn't get him out of her mind.

Back home, she quickly fell asleep. In her first dream, she was seeing Mr. Anand with his playful smile talking to her in his soft voice. Then she had another dream, where Rakesh's face would be replaced with the face of Varun. Both men had so little in common, she had met them both in the hospital, but Rakesh is so much better than Varun ever was. Varun… he had potential but, in the end, he let her down. Mr. Anand wouldn't let her down. She could tell this already.

Karishma woke up feeling rested despite her long shift, but she couldn't quite shake her dream. Why was she seeing Rakesh and Varun in a similar way? It bothered her, but she pushed it to the back of her mind. Karishma thought that food can bring her some comfort, so she went to her favorite spot.

***

The food place was just downstairs from her apartment. They had the best akuri in the whole town and it always brightened Karishma's mood. Plus, the owner, Raj, a chubby Punjabi guy was always fun to talk with. Raj was somewhere around his fifties with a big belly and a kind smile. If he was a bit younger and a bit less round, Karishma could even give him a shot. When she was entering the shop, she noticed an elegant lady quickly leaving the shop with a big smile.

"Hola Raj," Karishma greeted the owner, "I missed your akuri so much," she smiled to him. Raj looked extremely radiant today, and Karishma started to suspect that maybe the woman she just saw had something to do with it

"Ah Karishma darling, did you see this pretty lady you passed in the doors? She is one of my regulars. I finally got the courage to ask her out…," Raj smiled, "and she said yes!" he seemed very content while he started to prepare her order.

She and Raj chatted for a while but this day they were both distracted. On any other day they would talk about life, love and work but today Karishma felt like she wants to be on her own. Raj was kind of father figure for her and he was the one to comfort her when things with Varun didn't go well. Her family was far away, and they were not really interested in her feelings, more they cared about the regularity of money transfers from her. Raj was her friend, but it was too early to tell him about Rakesh. She ate quickly and went to rest.

***

The next day Karishma was back at work, this time perfectly on time. She rushed through her daily routine anxiously anticipating the moment to see Rakesh. When she finished her quick rounds and was heading to finally take care of Mr. Anand, Doctor Patwari stopped her in the hall.

"Karishma, you look tired…" Doctor Patwari commented, "Maybe that double shift was too long for you. I think it would be best if we take our VIP client off your plate for today. We need to make sure he gets A+ treatment."

Karishma felt anger rising from her belly. Does he want to take her Rakesh away from her? That would be unacceptable. She decided to fight for her special patient, so she put on her nicest smile, arched her back and pushed her chest out as much as possible.

"No doctor, please don't worry. I always bring my A-game for our VIPs. I am up to the task." she looked at Doctor Patwari seductively.

His eyes started to wander from her face to her breasts. They lingered there as he mumbled, "Make sure it is A+ service. A isn't good enough. Now get to it."

It was easier than she thought. She scurried off before Doctor Patwari could change his mind and went straight to Rakesh's room. He greeted her with a wide grin.

"I missed you yesterday." he said.

"Do you really mean this?" Karishma wanted to ask him but instead she said, "Well, I'm here now. Can I help you with anything?" she finished with a big smile.

"I need some help changing into clean clothes. I can't manage it with the leg yet." He said, trying to get up.

Karishma grabbed an extra gown from the cupboard and went to help him up. She gave him her hand. When he put his hand in hers, shivers ran through her body. His touch felt so good against her skin that she could barely breathe. She tried to focus back on her job. "The nurse Navjot was supposed to help me last night… but I guess she just got distracted with something else." He said, but he didn't seem to be angry with Navjot.

Karishma smiled. She felt overjoyed that he needed her. She was sure that only she can give him the best care, definitely better than Navjot. He held his hands up and Karishma took his gown off to reveal his well-toned body. He had obviously been working out and Karishma had to fight the temptation to touch his abs. She helped him into the new hospital gown.

She wanted to stay there the whole day, but other tasks were waiting so she reluctantly left Rakesh.

***

As Karishma went about her duties at the hospital, she thought about the electric feeling of Rakesh's touch. Before she got too lost in her thoughts she was interrupted by Vinita at the coffee machine.

"Ooh! C'mon girl, I need to tell you something," she pulled Karishma towards one of the staff rooms.

"You know last night I was prepping Mr. Brendon for bed and I saw his dick. It was huge!" Vinita giggled.

"What is it with you and huge dicks?" Karishma asked amused.

"No, I'm serious. I wasn't expecting that so when I saw it I said to him – Yikes, Mr. Brendon you have a big package" Vinita continued.

"You said that? You know you can't talk to patients like that, he could have reported you!" Karishma said with disbelief.

"Oh, c'mon, that old pervert likes it. Do you know what he replied? He said 'Yeah I was a hunk back in my time. Girls used to love me" She imitated Mr. Brendon's Texan accent.

"You're crazy Vinita," Karishma said with a laugh.

"Yeah and then he said - too bad it doesn't get hard anymore. Maybe little Brendon needs some young touch," Vinita continued with blushed cheeks.

"Seriously?" Karishma asked startlingly.

"I swear! And you know what I did?" Vinita continued "I grabbed it and gave it a couple of strokes and that old farts dick started to get hard in my hands instantly! His little Brendon wasn't little at all." She chuckled loudly.

Karishma was stunned hearing what Vinita said. She looked at her with disbelief while Vinita laughed uncaringly. Normally, Karishma would have never believed what Vinita just told her, but after seeing her that night with Doctor Patwari she knew what Vinita was capable of.

"Are you crazy?" Karishma's voice got more serious, "You'll get yourself into trouble."

"Why? Well, he is going to die soon. I just thought I should give him some last pleasures," Vinita said coldly "Maybe I will fuck him before he dies. That's kind of charity" she added with a mischievous smile.

"Vinita, behave!" Karishma said with disgust. "I am going to check on the motorbike patient." She could still hear Vinita's laughter as she walked down the hall.

Karishma didn't really care, Vinita was an adult. All that Karishma cared at this very moment was her new patient so she went to check on him again, but he was asleep. She went close to him and started looking at his face. "He is stunning," Karishma thought. She could kiss his beautiful lips right now. At once she regretted not having confidence like Vinita; "If it was Vinita instead of me, she would have done it by now," she thought to herself. She wanted to touch his flawless face and kiss him all over, but she knew she couldn't. He was her patient. And being a nurse is a responsibility, personal feelings can't affect the professional life.

The only time she broke that rule, it ended badly for everyone. Varun wasn't as stunning as Rakesh, not by a long shot, but he had charm and confidence. She always liked how Varun made the first move. He was the only guy to really make her feel special… too bad he was also amazing at making her feel terrible. She knew he regretted it, so that chapter of romance was closed.

Rakesh started to stir and blinked his eyes open.

"Time to wake up sleepyhead!" Karishma instantly felt like a nerd saying something like that.

"Are you sure? Maybe you were checking me out naked." Rakesh said with a stern look on his face.

"No, I wasn't. I swear!" She told him terrified thinking if this was possible that he was reading her mind.

"Relax! I was just messing around with you." Rakesh told her with a mischievous smile. "Karishma is an uncommon name. I haven't heard it before." He looked into her eyes.

"It is. I haven't heard it a lot either." Karishma felt like she was on a date and could swear he was flirting with her. She felt the blood flowing to her face and her heart was beating faster. She knew she shouldn't feel like this about a patient, but she couldn't help herself. And it felt right; it felt like she belonged here, with Rakesh.

"Are you married Karishi?" He moved to more personal questions.

"Single," she replied quietly, secretly liking that he was calling her 'Karishi.' No one ever called her like that before. It was like Rakesh was creating a secret language for only two of them.

"So how has some lucky guy not put a ring on it yet? A pretty girl like you shouldn't be alone." He was even more flirtatious now.

Karishma brushed off his compliment. "I'm sure you tell all the nurses that."

"Darling, you are the only nurse I want to see around me, the only one here that I like. I really like you, Karishi. You are pretty and professional, the rare combination really," he said looking deeply into her eyes. All Karishma could do was blush and smile shyly. She knew she should stop staring at him, but she couldn't. He didn't stop looking cheekily at her either. There was so much electricity at that moment that any second longer she would jump and kiss him. The beeper in her pocket vibrated, bringing her back to reality.

"Sorry Sir, I have to check on this," she scurried out of the room, trying to collect herself after their powerful moment.

"Rakesh flirted with me! He is definitely as into me as I am into him." she thought. She was paged to check Mr. Brendon's room. His room reeked of cheap cologne. Karishma wondered what that old pervert would need from her.

She was barely through the door when Mr. Brendan yelled, "You're not Vinita. Where is my Vinita?"

"She isn't your Vinita Mr. Brendan. She is a nurse, and so am I. What can I help you with?" She tried not to sound annoyed.

"Well, I want Vinita. She made me a promise." Mr. Brendan shouted with his Texan accent.

"Sorry, she's busy. I will tell her to come and see you when she is available," Karishma told him happy that she can leave the room.

"Actually, you can help me with something. Come here" he requested.

Karishma didn't want to, but she thought it would be quicker to get rid of him if she pretended she cared. When she moved closer, he grabbed her hand and pulled her towards him.
"That Vinita woke up something in me. Got the 'ole cock and balls working again. Now you gotta finish the job." he whispered in her ear. Karishma was stunned.

"You dirty old man! I don't care what that slut Vinita told you, but that is not how you talk to a nurse or any woman. If it were up to me I would have you thrown out of the hospital!" She pulled her arm from his hands. She immediately regretted her words. Mr. Brendon was one of the VIP patients.

Mr. Brendon grabbed his crotch and thrust his pelvis at her. "The sexy nurse said she would suck this. You don't have an ass like her, but this dick isn't gonna suck itself! C'mon, I know all you nurses are sluts and I'm a big deal 'round here. Do it or you will regret it!"

Karishma was so horrified she stormed out of the room. She found Vinita sitting in the staff room alone. Her fellow nurse was smiling until she saw the look on Karishma's face.

"That old pervert of yours is out of hand!" Karishma started angrily.

"Whoa! Calm down Kari, what happened?" Karishma's serious face startled Vinita.

"Mr. Brendon tried to get a handjob from me. This is a hospital, not a whore house," Karishma surprised herself with how passionate she was. She had gotten angry over patients misbehaving before, but this felt more personal.

"That silly old man, he really thought I would suck his dick," Vinita said with a cunning laugh. "Relax Kari. he's harmless. He wasn't taking his pills, so I told him that I would suck him off if he took his pills. No big deal," Vinita smirked.

This hardly satisfied Karishma. "Yes, it is a big deal! You could get fired for saying things like that." She tried to calm herself. Vinita was crazy, but Mr. Brendan crossed the line, not her.

"Don't worry about him, worse comes to worst I will suck Doctor Patwari's dick. He won't do anything to me," she said jokingly with a laugh.

"You are unbelievable," Karishma spat the words out angrily. Sometimes the language that Vinita was using was so vulgar and obscene that Karishma was thinking why she was even friend with her.
"I don't want to deal with this man ever again," she added.

Vinita made a teasing face, "You're saying he wanted you? Oh my god! Brendon betrayed me. I thought he loved me," she raised her hands in a dramatic gesture. "Ok, ok, sorry Kari. Don't worry about it. I will handle him" Vinita sounded decent for the first time.

"You better," The ice was finally leaving Karishma's voice.

"Maybe you are just stressed because you have to deal with that jerk with the broken leg?" Vinita asked the question in the form of a statement.

"Who? Rakesh?" Karishma could not believe these words. He was the best patient ever. Why would Vinita ever call him a jerk?

"Whatever his name is. I had to take care of him last night while you were off, and he was so rude. One-word answers, not even looking at me." Vinita rolled her eyes to emphasize how annoyed she was.

"Was he? Really?" Karishma wasn't angry anymore. She just wanted to hear the rest of Vinita's story.

"Yeah! I tried to make him interested in me, you know. Just to kill time. So, I showed off the girls. You know, I bent over with the top button undid and the usual stuff. But he really didn't care. I think he's gay," Vinita said. "Anyway, Kari, don't worry about Brandon and ignore the one leg jerk. My shift is finally done." She packed her bag, blew Karishma a kiss and left.

Her words stuck with Karishma for the rest of the day. Vinita was always getting all the attention. Why would Rakesh ignore her? She knew Vinita wasn't lying because she was visibly annoyed. She wasn't used to men ignoring her. Did that mean that Rakesh really could like a girl like Karishma? Did he find her more attractive than he found Vinita? Karishma's heart was beaming with joy as she was thinking about it. After summing up all the facts, she was certain he was different than Varun and that there is a future for them. All she had to do was figure out how to make it happen.

***

On the way home, Karishma stopped by her favorite food place. Seeing Raj instantly made her feel better.

"Why the long face? Is it anything my handmade mango chutney can't cure?" he teased.

Karishma smiled. She always felt comfortable around Raj, like a big brother or an uncle.

"Just guy problems." She sighed.

"Ah, a new man in your life? Why haven't you brought him by yet? I would give him my extra spicy salsa, so we can see what he is really made of." Raj joked while cutting some veggies.

"Hahaha, no new man. Just… potential I guess. Just not sure if it's worth it. He is from the hospital. I just don't want to make the same mistakes as before." She lied, she knew Rakesh was worth it, and she would try her best to get him. This time she should be luckier than with Varun.

Raj slid a deliciously smelling plate of akuri over to Karishma and sat down with her. "Sounds like you are getting a little bit ahead of yourself. Just relax and let things happen, if they happen. I always try to rush things and that's probably why I don't have a miss helping me with the shop."

Karishma shook her head, "I'm just worried that things might turn out like last time. You remember, I told you about him. He was also a patient. I knew I shouldn't have, but he was so sweet and charming, and I thought the world of him. He was almost perfect, then he went and ruined everything, He cheated on me." She hung her head over the akuri plate, "And later just disappeared."

"Whoa now girl, you are already worried if a guy will cheat on you and you aren't even together yet. Relax. Take things slowly. keep it casual. Good things happen that way." Raj smiled.

Karishma thought he might have a point. Maybe she was getting ahead of herself. Everything with Varun happened so fast and it went so wrong. Maybe this time she should try to be more casual and not try too hard.

Chapter 3

"Nurse Karishma. Report to the admin office immediately," the voice from the loudspeaker sent shivers down Karishma's spine. She had just clocked in and already things were going wrong. She rushed into the elevator and hit the top button. The admin office was always trouble. They only called someone there for disciplinary actions.

Doctor Patwari greeted her in the admin office. "Karishma, we have a very serious issue here. A patient made some very disturbing allegations about you."

Karishma was stunned. She instantly thought about Rakesh. Maybe she had been flirting too much.

"Yesterday you were sent to assist with Mr. Brendan. He says he woke up and found you rifling through his drawers and trying to steal money from him. We take theft very seriously at Saint Garance Hospital, especially when it is against one of our esteemed donors." Doctor Patwari had a very serious look on his face.

Karishma was stunned at the accusation. "Doctor Patwari. This is ridiculous. I have worked here for almost four years and never had an issue like this."

Doctor Patwari sighed, "Regardless Karishma, this is a very serious claim. The hospital will have to do a thorough investigation. Sadly, until the investigation is complete, you will be suspended without pay."

Karishma sat in silence for a second. Not only could she lose her job, but she could lose her chance with Rakesh. She couldn't let this happen. She stood up angrily.

"Doctor, you should know that horrible old man is a filthy pervert. You know it and I know it!" she gasped quickly.

Doctor shook his head. "That doesn't change anything."

"But he harassed me…He told me I had to do Mukhamaithun on him or he would make trouble for me." Karishma was getting more and more defensive.

Doctor Patwari let out a heavy sigh, "Mr. Brendan may have made a few inappropriate comments but that doesn't mean anything. Just means he made a few bad jokes. And his allegations still must be investigated."

Karishma was getting desperate. She couldn't let this go wrong. Without thinking she yelled angrily, "Vinita promised she would suck him off if he took his pills and now he is thrusting his genitals at other nurses and making rampant accusations."

Doctor's eyes grew wide, "Vinita… that couldn't be. She wouldn't."

"You know Vinita. Especially you should know what kind of girl she really is." Karishma realized she was treading into dangerous waters. She stopped herself from saying more and stared at the doctor.

"What is that supposed to mean? What are you insinuating?" his face turned bright red. She didn't know if that was because he got angry or scared.

"I just meant that you know how she teases and flirts with the patients. That's all." She felt that this answer was good enough to ease the situation.

Doctor Patwari gave her a hard stare. "Maybe you should head home before you say anything you might regret later. We will be in touch after we have investigated further."

Karishma felt shattered. She could lose her job, she could lose her best friend at work and she could lose Rakesh all at once. She tried to keep the tears from coming as she fled the hospital. It wasn't fair, nothing in this situation was fair, and now she would pay the highest price.

***

After a few hours of tears, and she finally settled down and dried her eyes. Her phone buzzed. It was Vinita. Karishma reluctantly picked it up.

"What the hell did you say? What did you do? I don't give a shit what other people think about me in this hospital, but I thought you were different. I thought you were my friend!" Vinita shouted to the phone. Karishma could barely sneak in a word.

"But Vinita, Doctor Patwari was so angry, saying I would be suspended and fired," she tried to explain by talking over enraged friend.

Vinita didn't let her finish, "It doesn't matter. You backstabber! You two-faced, fake friend! How dare you repeat what I tell you as a friend to the admin. You of all people?! How could you do this, Karishma?"

"I didn't repeat anything, I promise. I just said that Mr. Brendon was harassing me, I never…"

Vinita stopped her, "I don't want to hear your lies. I never thought you would be the traitor to backstab me like this. Go to hell, Kari." The phone went dead. Karishma felt so alone. She found herself on her laptop typing Rakesh Anand into the google search bar, wondering what could have been. She was no stranger to snooping online. She used to check on Varun all the time, that's how she found out about who he really was.

Private Facebook. No Twitter. No Instagram. "How is this guy not on more social media?" she wondered. She looked up a few articles about his business. He was more successful than she thought – there were lots of articles about his work and company. He studied in London and worked hard to build a little empire. Karishma felt excited thinking about being part of his life and how she would prove her family that she is something more than the monthly money transfer. She fell asleep dreaming about that smile and what could have been.

Chapter 4

She woke up to the voicemail light blinking on her phone.

"Karishma. It looks like the situation with Mr. Brendan was a big misunderstanding. We would like to still come in this evening for your originally scheduled shift."

Karishma's mind raced as she tried to figure out exactly what that meant. There was no way an administrative complaint could have been cleared up that quickly, so someone must have backed up her story. Maybe Vinita decided to come clean about what she had said to this old perv? She ran through all the possible scenarios as she got to the hospital. As she headed back to the nurses' office she spotted Vinita.

"Vinita, can we talk?" she asked.

"What do you want, backstabber?" Her friend didn't seem open to any conversation.

"I just want to say… thank you. I don't know what you said to Doctor Patwari, but..."

"What did I say to Doctor Patwari? What I said?" Vinita yelled angrily. "You said more than enough for both of us. He was so angry with me he was shouting all afternoon. If he didn't love staring at this ass he would have fired me right then and there." Vinita scoffed.

"So, you didn't say anything about me?" Karishma tried to make sense out of the situation.

"After you threw me under the bus? Why would I? I only help my friends." Vinita pushed past her and went out.

Karishma was very confused. If Vinita hadn't helped her, then why had Doctor Patwari let her come back? Before her thoughts could run any further, she heard her name being paged over the PA again. "What now?" she thought.

She headed to Doctor Patwari's office. He looked even grumpier than usual, too grumpy to even stare at her breasts.
"The situation we discussed yesterday is a serious issue, and just because we allowed you to come back does not mean it's over." Doctor sternly said.

"I understand Doctor."

"There will still be an investigation, but into his allegation and yours. Normally I wouldn't put up with any of this nonsense. If I fully believed Mr. Brandon's story, you would be out of this hospital. You're lucky you have a good Deva with friends in high places. As far as I am concerned, you will only be given a warning. And, of course, you won't have to attend Mr. Brandon anymore" The doctor rubbed his temple and shook his head.

Karishma was relieved but also confused. What friends could she have that would help her… "Good Deva? But who? Vinita?" she asked.

"Looks like you did a good job with our VIP patient in room 23B. He heard some nurses gossiping about you and called his friend on the board. I'm sick of talking about this. We don't need to have any more sexual harassment stories around here. Get back to work and stay out of trouble or, god forbid, not even the board can save you." Doctor turned his back on Karishma.

She had never seen Doctor Patwari so stressed, but she couldn't get his words out of her head, "room 23B patient." So it was Rakesh who saved her! He was her good Deva. It's not her imagination, he really cared about her. He was her knight. She was surprised yet flattered, confused, yet happy. Not even her closest friend at the hospital helped her, only her dear Rakesh. They had flirted a bit sure, and she couldn't get over how gorgeous he was, but why would he help her? It must be because he genuinely cared, she thought. Whatever it was, no man had ever done anything that nice for her, not even Varun.

She knocked on room 23B's door and entered the room. She saw her savior sitting on the bed, eating his soup while nurse Navjot was standing beside him with a napkin. He stopped eating when he looked at Karishma.

"Oh hey, now I have my two favorite nurses here," he said with a smile. "I'm glad to see you."

"Hello, Rakesh." She was rarely this casual with patients, but she felt safer with him now. "I heard you made some calls about me..." Karishma continued.

"Ah, it was nothing. I was just chatting with my golfing buddy, and he just happens to be one of the big wigs here. He's the reason I got this fancy room. I just told him how nice all the nurses here are treating me." Rakesh smiled at Navjot and Karishma.

Karishma with the corner of the eye she noticed that Navjot was giving her an awkward look. There was so much more she wanted to say, but not in front of Navjot.

Navjot abruptly jumped into the conversation, "You are saying nice things about us then? Who knew you were such a charmer!"

All of a sudden Karishma felt jealousy running through her veins. She wanted a moment alone with him, to thank him for his protection. No man ever did things like that for her and she felt this special connection between them. But she was patient. She would get him alone, just not quite yet...

***

The sun was low in the sky, but it was still quite warm. Karishma found herself sitting in a large antique chair in front of an ornate mirror. She ran a brush through her hair as she admired the peaceful, happy woman staring back at her. A silk expensive sari hugged her body.

"You are looking gorgeous, my love." She heard from behind. She turned around and saw Rakesh in a fancy black suit with a big grin on his face. Karishma smiled sweetly back, looking at this unbelievably beautiful man while she played with the large wedding ring on her finger.

Rakesh came close to her and embraced her. Their lips locked in an intense and romantic kiss. He slowly brushed his hand against her back, sliding it down to her waist. He broke the kiss and grabbed her hand, leading her down the hall.

Karishma was in a beautiful house, exactly like she had always wanted, old fashioned with large windows overlooking the amazing garden full of colorful flowers. It was the perfect house to share with her perfect man. Rakesh pulled her towards the bedroom, but she held back.

"What's the matter?" Rakesh was surprised.

"Are the kids asleep?" She asked preoccupied.
"Yes, I tucked them in," Rakesh replied with a proud father's smile.

Karishma imagined him tucking in their angelic little children as she let him guide her to the bedroom. She found the bed covered with a silky white bedspread and rose petals thrown all around it. Candles flickered along the side tables and cast dancing shadows onto the walls.

"It's so beautiful, Rakesh," She said, looking at the romantically decorated room.

Rakesh brought his lips closer to Karishma's ear and whispered in her ear. "I love you."

Karishma looked back at him and hugged him tightly. "I love you too, my dear."

Rakesh swept her from her feet and carried her to the bed. He carefully laid her down and climbed onto the bed next to her. They kissed deeply. She was so lost in the kiss that she had to throw her arms around his neck for support. Without breaking the kiss, Rakesh slowly started to unwrap silk sari from her body. He kissed her neck, then her shoulder, lingering slowly around her collar bone with the tip of his tongue. Then he brought his lips back to hers.

Rakesh leaned back and started unbuttoning his shirt. Karishma watched as his bronzed chest was slowly revealed. He moved towards her and helped her out of her sari. She laid in front of him completely naked and defenseless. He leaned over and started kissing her on her forehead, then her lips, then chest, going more south to her belly button. And finally, he kissed Karishma on her warm wet spot in between her legs. "Oh, Rakesh!" Karishma drowned into an ocean of pleasure.

"Lay back and relax," Rakesh told her, and Karishma obliged. She put her head on the pillow and closed her eyes. She felt Rakesh's tongue on her labia. A jolt of pleasure ran through her body. Rakesh kissed the top of her vagina then licked in between Karishma's labia. Karishma felt another jolt. Rakesh's tongue explored her gently and finally settled onto licking her clitoris. He started to rapidly flick it with his tongue, resulting in Karishma unease and pleasure. Karishma grabbed her breast with one hand and laid the other hand on Rakesh's head, encouraging him to go on. Rakesh ran his tongue from the bottom to the top of her pussy, then moved back to her clit.

Karishma felt the warmth building up inside her. "Don't stop, oh God don't stop!" She moaned. Rakesh moved his tongue around her clitoris then he gently slid two fingers inside of her. Karishma's body trembled with so much pleasure that she almost forgot to breathe. Rakesh started moving his fingers in and out of her while he continued to lick her shishnika. The pleasure was too much for Karishma. The great pressure building inside her quickly released while Rakesh licked and vigorously fingered her. She sighed with pleasure and looked at her still hungry man. It was amazing yoni lehan.

He looked at her saying "You taste amazing."

Karishma smiled at him, "that was incredible." she said, "now it's your turn."

His pants were off in a flash and he looked down at her spread legs and freshly eaten vagina. She was amazed at how hard and large his penis was. If she wasn't so wet from his tongue, there is no way it would fit in her. Rakesh grabbed his erection and moved towards her.

"Put it in," she commanded, and Rakesh obliged. He started slowly just rubbing his head on the opening of her vagina and then pushed his entire length inside with a single thrust. Karishma bit her lip to keep herself from screaming. Rakesh was seeming to enjoy it as well, as he closed his eyes and moving swiftly in and out of her while moaning.

"You are so wet, my love." he said.

"You made me wet." she whispered.

Rakesh grabbed her breast and squeezed it gently. Karishma felt the warmth building inside of her again. She locked her legs around Rakesh's waist and tried to pull him even deeper into her. Karishma could tell he was about to finish from the look on his face.

"Please love, cum inside me," Karishma said as she felt herself moving closer to another climax. Their hips moved together as one body until finally Rakesh filled her up with his hot love juice. Rakesh could feel her vagina's contraction sucking inside all his cum. He gently slid off from her and looked deep into her eyes. "I love you," Karishma said to Rakesh.

"I love you too, my dearest." He replied in a soothing, warm voice.

The alarm clock rang and Karishma woke from the most beautiful dream she ever had. She pressed the snooze hoping that the dream would continue. She started to drift into the dream world again. Karishma found herself crumpled on the ground in a dark empty room in front of a big wooden door. No matter how hard she pulled, it wouldn't budge an inch. She fell to her knees in despair, but someone's hand rested on her shoulder. She looked up to see Rakesh standing beside like her good Deva. He opened the door easily and light filled the room. She fell into his arms sobbing and thanking him. His arms enveloped her in a giant hug and she never felt safer.

She looked to his face and was met with a soft gentle kiss. Her heart raced as she closed her eyes and fully embraced the kiss.

When she opened her eyes again it wasn't Rakesh holding her but Varun. His unshaven hipster look, that she used to like so much, was no longer appealing at all compared to Rakesh's chiseled chin. She struggled to pull away from him, but he didn't want to let her go. Suddenly he pushed her to the ground and slammed the door shut, plunging her back into the oppressive darkness.

Karishma woke in a cold sweat to the incessant beeping of her alarm. Varun's pale face was still sharp in her memory. She couldn't figure out why Varun kept intruding into her thoughts. She was done with him, he would never return. Still, he dared to hunt her in her dreams. It came to her mind that maybe Varun wanted to warn her not to make the same mistakes with Rakesh as she did with him. This time she will do things right. She will take Raj's advice. Keep it casual, let things happen naturally.

Chapter 5

The dream lingered in her mind through the beginning of her shift until she finally got to check on Rakesh.

He was lying in bed watching daytime TV. His smile when she entered the room made her instantly forget all the stress of the day before.

"Can't you guys get anything decent like HBO in here?" Rakesh joked as Karishma started checking his blood pressure.

"Maybe you should talk to your friend on the board about that," Karishma quipped back with a wink. Rakesh looked with amusement in his eyes and softly grabbed her hand. She felt shocks of pleasure throughout her body when he touched her. She matched his gaze and blushed, smiling timidly.

Without breaking eye contact, Rakesh softly asked, "Is everything alright Karishi?"

"Yes," was all Karishma could answer. She was feeling overwhelmingly nervous. The way Rakesh was looking at her left little doubt in her mind that he was interested… very interested. But she didn't want to rush things. She wanted to let them unfold, keep it casual. Not make the same mistakes as last time… But his strong hand felt so good on hers.

"I didn't get a chance to properly thank you yesterday." she finally broke eye contact and looked to the ground.

"It's really nothing, Karishma." He said, "I like how you take care of me."
She blushed and pulled her hand back. Her world was spinning and the way he was looking at her made her feel wanted. This was different from the pervy looks that doctor Patwari gave her. This was real. She wanted to just grab him and kiss him right then.

Then his phone rang. He grabbed it quickly while muttering, "Son of a bitch… she always calls at the worst times."

He hesitated and looked at Karishma awkwardly, then back at the phone. For a moment Karishma froze. They had such a powerful moment and he would end it just for a phone call? She huffed to show how annoyed she was and walked out of the room.

She paused just outside the door and heard him answered but it was too quiet to hear anything. Then she heard his voice clearly as he started to yell into his phone.

"You don't even come back to the country? Do you even care that I had an accident? What about the kids? They aren't coming either? What kind of family is this? What kind of wife are you?" He yelled into the phone.

Karishma felt sick – thousands of thoughts were running through her head. Rakesh has a wife? He has children? Why does it feel like with Varun all over again? Was Varun in her dream trying to warn her? She remembered very well when Varun cheated on her. She spent all day in a car in front of his house just to find out that he was cheating on her with some French student whore, Eloise, sweet Eloise. And now with Rakesh she felt the same - betrayed and deceived.

Karishma barely remembered coming home from work. She fell into a heap on the floor and contemplated how everything could have gone so wrong. She didn't take things too fast, she didn't do anything wrong. He cared, he liked her, and he wanted her. She saw it in his eyes. Then she finds out he has a wife.

"Maybe I just got too ahead of myself. I was already planning our wedding," she thought. "What if he doesn't love his wife anymore? He's an adult and adults fall in and out of love." The spark of hope started to shine through the darkness. "Maybe he doesn't love his wife. Maybe he likes me more than he likes his wife. Maybe he isn't happy with his married life." Her tired brain produced an endless list of excuses, but no matter how many excuses she made, she couldn't forget that he had a family.

The other voice in her head repeated that Rakesh was just another guy who tried to seduce her and get into her pants. "Maybe he just wants to have sex with me. Maybe everything he said was a lie, just to get me into bed. Maybe he tried to use me like all the other men that I have been with. Maybe my mother was right – there should be no sex before marriage, maybe I am a westernized slut." The second voice in her head repeated.

The internal fight was too much for her. She decided to sleep on it confront Rakesh the next day. She hoped her head would be clearer in the morning. That night she had nightmares about Rakesh and Varun.

In her dream, she walked into Rakesh's room and he was having sex with a beautiful, brown hair woman. Rakesh stared at Karishma with a mean grin as he pounded the blonde. Karishma screamed and

Rakesh started to laugh. She covered her eyes as the scream intensified.

When she opened her eyes, it was no longer Rakesh in the bed but Varun. Varun laid completely still, and the brown hair woman was nowhere to be seen. Karishma approached the bed and touched Varun's cheek. It was cold and clammy. She could tell he was dead. Karishma shuddered. She had already said goodbye to Varun, why did he keep haunting her?

Her dreams continued fitfully throughout the night.

***

Karishma stood outside of Rakesh's room hesitating over what to do next. She didn't know what to say or how to face him. She felt so foolish. She reached the room and decided to get in without knocking. She saw him sitting on the edge of his bed struggling to get a hospital gown over his cast. His muscular shoulders were bare and more tanned than Karishma imagined.

"Sorry, I didn't mean to barge in like that," Karishma said meekly avoiding looking at him in the eyes.

Rakesh with no hesitation put his hand on Karishma's shoulder for support and squeezed it just a little bit, sending jolts of pleasure throughout Karishma's body. His face was so close to her that she could feel his breath. Karishma tried to focus on her job and what she came to say, but Rakesh was making it hard. He was so close to her that she could feel the warmth of his body. She managed to put Rakesh into a gown and stepped as far away from him as she could.

"You disappeared yesterday. I was sad that you didn't come to visit me again. Karishi" Rakesh looked at her with a fake puppy dog face. At least Karishma thought it was fake.

"You didn't tell me you were married," Karishma stated abruptly surprising herself with the harness of the voice.

"No, I didn't tell you that," Rakesh admitted.
"You lied to me." Karishma fought back tears. This feeling in her stomach was just like the one she had when she found out about Varun's infidelity.

"I never lied, I just never explained my situation. It's more complicated than you think." he stammered, looking down.
Karishma had to admit to him that he was right. He never lied. He just didn't tell her, but he was still obviously flirting with her.

"It doesn't matter how complicated it is. How do you think your wife would react if she saw how you are with the nurses here?" Karishma put extra emphasis on the words 'your wife.'

"Listen, things are not good at home. They haven't been for a long time. Why do you think 'my wife' hasn't come to visit me? Things fell apart a long time ago, but we stayed together for the kids. It wouldn't be fair to them to break up the family. And anyway, how did you find out?" Rakesh tried to change the subject and make the mood more playful.

Karishma didn't want to admit that she was eavesdropping on his phone conversation, and it sounded like a heated argument. Maybe he was telling the truth. Maybe she misjudged a man like she had done with Varun before? Karishma was confused. He was right. And he definitely liked Karishma, so why not give him a chance? Everyone deserves a second chance, don't they?

"And that doesn't matter. I'm just happy I got to meet you. We're having a good time together and I'm getting much better. Isn't that all that matters?" Rakesh flashed his biggest and most charming grin.

Karishma was angry at herself for being so soft on him. She had planned how to confront him, what questions to ask and how to tell him off. Instead, he made her rethink everything. "I shouldn't be okay with this." she thought to herself. "Why am I even listening to him? Was this the same as what happened with Varun?" the thoughts were spinning in her mind. "Am I just destined to end up with cheaters and betrayers? Although nothing actually happened between Rakesh and I… But he has a wife and I wanted something to happen. And he did too."

"I'm sorry… I have to get back to work." She mumbled and backed out of the room with her mind racing.

"Karishma," Rakesh called.

Karishma looked back at him and said nothing.

"Does it matter?" he asked.

Karishma didn't know what to say. She left the room without saying anything to Rakesh. "Does it matter?" she asked herself the same question. "It should," Karishma thought. "But does it?"

The rest of the day she deliberated on what to do. She started to think that maybe it would be better to just trade patients and avoid the whole thing. Although, he had saved her. He probably saved her job. Karishma didn't know what to do.

***

At the end of her shift, she ran into Doctor Patwari.

"Are you keeping your good Deva happy?" he asked, winking.

Karishma felt like she would cry "I don't know. Maybe it's better if someone else takes care of him."

Doctor Patwari started to become angry. "What the hell Karishma? You get your ass saved a day ago and now you want to throw it away? No way. He asked for you specifically and now he gets you."

His angry yelling combined with the Rakesh situation was too much for Karishma. She burst into tears.

Doctor softened. "Listen, I know this has been tough for you. I'm not trying to be the bad guy, I just have to do what is best for the hospital."

Karishma looked up at him, "I know. I'm sorry. I will do better tomorrow."

Doctor Patwari put his hand on her shoulder. "You have a good Deva looking out for you. Don't worry too much but stop crying. It's ugly. Nobody likes an ugly nurse."

Karishma felt like crying all over again after his comment, but she kept it together and went home. Karishma felt like the pressure was building and she was about to explode. Her job was hanging by a thread, her best friend hates her, and she can't stop thinking about a patient who has a wife. Despite everything, Rakesh's smile was still in her mind. If he and his wife are just together for the kids, then maybe… She wished she wasn't attracted to him, but whenever she looked at him, her heart melted. All she could think about was his face, those muscular shoulders, and how she would love to be with him. How nice will it feel to kiss him? No matter what, she knew she would have to face him again the next day.

***

Mid-morning she realized she couldn't put it off anymore and went to Rakesh's room. He was in the middle of another heated phone conversation, but he gestured for her to stay.

"That was just the nurse coming in," Rakesh said on the phone. "Are the kids ok?"

Karishma couldn't help but wonder why he would want her to stay if he was talking to his wife.

"I told you already, my phone was on silent. I was sleeping. No, no. Just leave it alone." his voice started to rise in volume with each no.

"Listen, just tell the kids I'm ok and I miss them," Rakesh said. Then he looked at his phone with disgust and put it down.

"Sorry. She doesn't want the kids to come to see me," he said.

"Rakesh, I am just your nurse, I don't need to know your personal details." She said trying to stay firm and not start crying.

"They are in London, some cousin's wedding. I guess she told them my accident wasn't bad, so they won't worry but now I just feel like they don't care." Rakesh answered.

Karishma wondered how could possibly be enjoying her cousin's wedding when her husband was in hospital. "If he were my husband, I would never leave him alone, even for a second." Karishma thought.

"Listen, I know you were a bit surprised yesterday. I feel bad. I've had a hard time even before the accident. It feels good to have someone take such good care of me. Especially someone so beautiful." Saying this he looked at her again with the eyes of a puppy.

Karishma wasn't used to a compliment like this. It made her feel special. She immediately felt sorry for him. She could see how much this was bothering him and she wanted to help him, to show that she cared for him as well. All she wanted now was to hug him and kiss him and tell him how special he is. "If his wife doesn't care that he is in the hospital then they must be pretty much apart," she thought. "No wonder he was looking for love and affection," Karishma thought and felt like a huge weight off her shoulders.

"Anyways," Rakesh shook his head. "You didn't answer my question earlier."

"What question?" She asked.

"Does it matter that I am married? I's just for the kids you know." He replied while staring deep into her eyes.

Karishma had to look away, "I don't know."

Rakesh nodded "I understand. Can you bring me my water?"
She brought a glass of water to him but instead of taking it, he softly took her hand. Karishma's heart skipped a couple of heartbeats. She tried to free her hand from his grip, but he was holding it tight.

"Let me go," Karishma said in a shallow and unconvincing tone. Rakesh pulled her closer to him until Her face was just inches away from his. His hot breath tickled her cheek. She looked at Rakesh's lips as he started to bring them closer to hers. Part of her was telling her to get away from him, but the rest of her wanted it more than anything else.

"I want you to know how special you are and that I appreciate what you are doing for me. You are making me feel comfortable for the first time in so long." He whispered as he stared into her eyes.

His face was so close to her that she could smell his skin. Rakesh brought his lips closer to her, and she kissed him willingly. She felt her lips touch his and she could hear her heartbeat pounding in her ears. His lips were smooth, tender and delicious. Karishma could kiss him all day. She felt Rakesh's hand on her waist trying to get inside her dress. That brought her back to her senses and with the last gasp of the free will, Karishma pulled away before he could get any further. She stood speechless, looking at Rakesh and thinking about what just happened. Rakesh was looking back at her sitting on his bed, with a sexy smile on his face.

"I knew it didn't matter," He said with a seductive tone.

Karishma fled towards the door. Before leaving she took a fleeting glance back to see Rakesh grinning. She smiled as well then left without a word.

Chapter 6

Karishma reached the hospital and changed into her nursing uniform. She was anxious to see Rakesh but, at the same time, very conflicted over the whole situation. She walked by Doctor Patwari and tried to avoid his prying eyes.

"Hello, Doctor," She said, passing by.

"Oh, Karishma, good that you are here," He said. "First of all, it is nice to hear compliments about your work from the patients. Your friend from 23B praised you a lot. Secondly, we are understaffed in Neurology today. You will have to fill in."

"But doctor, can't someone else filled in?" She started to protest.

"What is it with you? Why do you second guess all my decisions recently? You can check on your patients here later. Navjot will cover you here." Doctor Patwari gave an exasperated sigh and walked away.

She contemplated sneaking off to see Rakesh before she started in Neurology, but she preferred not to cross Doctor Patwari again.

She had worked in the Neurology before, so she knew most of the staff and always liked working with them. She got assigned to support Doctor Wolfratberger. Doctor Wolfratberger was younger than most of the other doctors and much more handsome. All the other Neurology doctors were old, greying and mostly bald while Wolfratberger had neatly kept blonde hair and a cute German accent. He came to India from Europe to get some international experience and slowly was becoming the celebrity figure of the hospital – mostly because of his exotic look and implacable manners. Almost all the nurses had a crush on him, including Karishma – but now her crush was gone.

"Hello Doctor Wolfratberger," Karishma greeted him with a smile.

"Karishma, long time no see. Please, call me Franz" Compared to Doctor Patwari, Wolfratberger was much nicer to work with. And he didn't look at nurses' butts.

They exchanged pleasantries and got to work. Neurology was a slow department. Karishma liked the slower pace but soon found herself bored and her mind wandered to Rakesh. She wondered what he was doing and if he was thinking of her. She hoped Navjot wasn't bothering him, she was a nosy nurse and Karishma didn't particularly like her. Plus no one could take better care of him than herself.

She went to check on all the patients from room one to ten. Everything was fine, no one needed anything, so she came back to the empty staff room and drank tea. She wanted this shift to be over already, so she could go see Rakesh. Checking her watch, she saw she had one more hour until she could check on her man. Karishma found Doctor Wolfratberger just outside the staff room.

"Hello Doctor," she said.

"Franz, please. Call me Franz." he said with a kind smile.

"Ok, Franz." she replied. "Is there anything else you need? We are struggling with staff shortages in orthopedics and my help would be appreciated." Karishma looked at the steel blue eyes of Franz.

"I think everything is under control here. Just one thing..." he said as he moved closer to her.

"Yes, Franz?" she teased by trying to do a German accent by making "r" sound very pronounced.

"It's always a pleasure having you in the neurology ward," He said with a nervous look on his face. "Would you like to come to dinner with me sometime? It would be nice to get to know you away from the hospital."

Karishma was stunned. Doctor Wolfratberger was quite handsome and had this sensual European vibe that made him a great catch, but all she could think about was kissing Rakesh. She felt like even having a coffee with the doctor would be like cheating on her man. She did feel pretty good knowing the most sought-after doctor liked her. If only she could talk to Vinita about it, they would have quite the chat. Unless Vinita was sleeping with him also, she thought with a grimace.

"Oh, I am flattered Doctor Wolfratberger, really, but I don't think it's a good idea. I don't think it's proper to date within the hospital, even if we aren't in the same department." She knew it was a lie and felt a bit guilty. He was a good man, but now she had Rakesh.

"Oh, o-okay," Franz was visibly disappointed. Karishma knew that he wasn't expecting that. His face turned red with sadness, but he maintained his smile whatsoever.

"I'll go check on my patients now, Doctor Wolfratberger. Bye." Karishma said and went out of his office without looking back or giving him a chance to say anything more.

***

Karishma instantly wondered if she had made a terrible mistake. Doctor Wolfratberger was handsome. Plus, he was a Doctor and she never got any attention from the doctors other than Patwari's lecherous stares. She had turned him down because of a kiss with a married man! The guilty feeling came back stronger than before. She thought for a second that maybe she was as bad as Varun. She wasn't a cheater, but a home-wrecker. Was that any better?

She was scolding herself inside her head when she reached room 23B. She knocked on the door, entered and found Rakesh moving around awkwardly on his crutches. Even though he was very fit and coordinated, crutches make everyone look awkward. She smiled despite herself and quickly forgot all her doubts.

"See, I am making progress," Rakesh joked with Karishma.

"It's very good indeed," Karishma said with a bit of a giggle.

"You disappeared on me again yesterday. I was lonely." He teased with a wink.

"Oh, I am sure Navjot took good care of you," she said hoping he would disagree.

"But Navjot isn't you," Rakesh replied fast, sitting back on his bed.

Karishma felt a strange kind of tension in the room. She sat down on a seat and looked at Rakesh while he stared back with deep, hungry eyes. At this hour, the hospital was quiet and empty. Rakesh kept staring at her with a slight smile and wanting eyes. She felt excited and she sat down next to the bed. She tried not to look at his perfectly kissable lips.
"Why don't we sleep?" Rakesh asked, breaking the silence.

"What? I'm at work. I can't just sleep." The question stunned Karishma.

"I can't sleep worrying that you will disappear again. Just sleep in the chair. I'll wake you up if I need you." His playful smile pulled at her, enticing her closer.
"I am in enough trouble with his hospital already," Karishma said. "Let me get you your meds."

She stood and turned her back on Rakesh to sort out the smorgasbord of pills. Despite the leg and cast, Rakesh gracefully pulled himself out of the bed and stood directly behind her. He wrapped his thick, muscular arms around her and pulled her close to him in a great embrace. Karishma had to decide; either get out of the room or stay let destiny happen. Karishma knew this was trouble, but she couldn't leave. He was too intoxicating. She needed it to happen, she wanted to prove that she wasn't crazy thinking that he wants her too. And maybe this is what Raj meant when he said to keep it casual. There were no promises, no words spoken, just raw sexual energy.

She ambled towards the switchboard, and she could feel Rakesh grabbing on to her from behind. As she turned the lights off, Rakesh started kissing her neck. Karishma melted into his arms. She leaned her head back against him and Rakesh kissed her neck passionately. Her heart was beating fast, and her legs were trembling. Rakesh grabbed Karishma's breast from behind and squeezed them gently.

She moaned in Rakesh's ear, "Oh Rakesh." She felt him growing in his pants as he pressed it against her ass. She turned around to face him and stared him in the eye. They locked their lips into a gentle but deep kiss. Rakesh slid his tongue into her mouth. Karishma welcomed his tongue with her own. Meanwhile, Rakesh's hands were exploring Karishma's body all over, from her hips to waist to her back. Karishma's grabbed his back and felt the sinewy muscles just under the skin. she pushed her body against him as hard as she could. Rakesh undid her buttons skillfully, and Karishma let her shirt fall off her onto the ground. He grabbed at her waistband and she helped him slide off the hospital pants. Rakesh broke the kiss and took two steps backward to admire Karishma's semi-nude body.

He smiled then deftly reached around her back and unclasped her bra. She felt shy for a moment with her breasts exposed and crossed her arms to cover them. Rakesh gently moved her hands aside and stared at them like he was gazing upon fine art. Karishma knew there was no way back from here. She took her panties off in a flash. She could see the hunger and lust in Rakesh's eyes and it turned her on even more, like throwing gasoline onto the fire inside her.

Karishma couldn't remember the last time she presented herself like this to anyone. She guessed it was Varun. The romance also started in a hospital, but they got physical much later. And it was nothing like this. Not like this crazy energy.

She grabbed at Rakesh's shirt saying, "It's your turn."

Rakesh smiled at her and stepped back. He undid the buttons of his shirt and took it off. He struggled a little because of one of his injured hand. She had to help him get his pants off with his injured leg; it wasn't the first time she saw him like this, but this time she knew she was going to see it all.

Karishma couldn't wait any longer and fell into his arms. The touch of her bare skin against his was electric. She kissed him aggressively as he grabbed her ass. Karishma had goosebumps all over her body. She could feel how hard he was when she rubbed her wet vagina against it. Rakesh took the hint and grabbed one of Karishma's hands and put it inside his underwear. Karishma touched Rakesh's penis for the first time. It was even bigger than she imagined. Vinita hadn't lied about that. And it was rock-hard. Karishma grabbed his manhood and gave it a couple of strokes before Rakesh pushed his underwear off. Their bare bodies intertwined so you could barely see where one ended and the other began.

Karishma couldn't take it anymore; she put the tip of Rakesh's penis on her wet vagina and started rubbing it. They both moaned simultaneously.

"Take me, Rakesh. Take me now." Karishma whispered in Rakesh's ear.

"You don't need to tell me twice," He teased as he picked her up with his good hand and laid her on the bed. He climbed on top of her and she could feel the head of his penis rubbing the inside of her thighs.

"Put it in, Rakesh, make me yours." She begged. Without hesitation, Rakesh pushed his manhood inside of her with one swift motion. Karishma was so wet that Rakesh's significant size slid in without any resistance. She moaned and felt like she was flying. Rakesh started moving in and out of her making her moan with every thrust of his penis. She tried to push against him to take it deeper.

Sex had never been like this for Karishma. Sure, it had felt good, but this was fireworks. This was magic. Rakesh quickened the pace and she could hardly breathe. He grabbed her breast while moving in and out.

Karishma could feel her orgasm building. "You are going to make me cum, Rakesh," her words escaped between ragged gasps of ecstasy.

"I'm close," he said between heavy breaths.

"Oh, Rakesh. Let's cum together." Karishma was losing herself in the moment. Rakesh held her from her hips and went faster than she thought was possible. Karishma knew he was about to cum, as she reached her climax. She grabbed the bedcovers hard and started to finish as she felt Rakesh ejaculate inside of her. They both moaned, and he rolled beside her, breathing heavily.

She laid her head on his chest. She felt so secure and safe with him that she didn't even care that she was in the hospital and someone could come in. All she cared about was being next to him. Karishma shut her eyes and drifted off to sleep. To her, this felt like home.

The next morning, she woke up slightly groggy and not sure if that was all a dream. Looking upon Rakesh's face solidified her in reality. She was so overjoyed that she just stared at his face for a moment. She looked over his chiseled jaw, the crest of his forehead, his smile lines, and those delicious lips. Rakesh slowly awoke to see Karishma staring at him. She shyly looked away and he laughed.

"Good morning, sleepyhead." He said with a joyful smile on his face.

"Good morning." She said coyly.

They had a quick kiss, then she slid out of bed to get dressed.
"You can't stay longer?" He asked with a whimsical look like if she stayed it all might happen again.

She knew she was already playing with fire, so she got dressed and snuck out of his room while Rakesh drifted back to sleep. She changed into her regular clothes and headed to the cafeteria. She sat on one of the empty tables and started having breakfast. She saw Vinita flirting with the cafeteria manager. It hurt to remember that they still weren't talking, but at that moment she didn't care. She was just happy that she had Rakesh.

Karishma felt like her dreams are finally coming true. Rakesh was different from other men she had been with. He was gentler and caring than anyone she ever met. Karishma had totally forgotten the fact that he was married, that he had kids, or the fact that she rejected a very eligible Doctor yesterday. She was just happy that things were the way they were.

Chapter 7

On the way home, she felt her phone vibrating. It was the reception from the hospital. "What now," she thought as she answered. "Karishma speaking."

The receptionist had a soft dreamy voice that kind of floated through the phone. "We just had a patient admitted and you were listed as the emergency contact."

"Who?" she nervously replied.

"Raj Singh. You know him?" the soft voice continued.

"Of course," Karishma answered nervously. "What happened to him?"

"He was found unconscious with erratic breathing. He is being treated now in the ER." The receptionist's voice seemed concerned.

Karishma turned around and headed back to the hospital. Even though she was exhausted, she had to check on Raj. He didn't have anyone else, so she had to be there for him. He was so kind and gentle to her that she didn't think twice about returning to the hospital immediately.

She hurried to the Emergency Room and asked the receptionist, "Where is Raj? Mr. Singh?"

"Third room on the left, he is in surgery," she answered.

Karishma rushed to the room, seeing through the glass that doctors were working on Raj. He was lying on the bed with a breathing mask over his face. Based on the receptionist's words and the heart surgeon being in the room, Karishma guessed he had a heart attack. A lifetime of hard work be hard on your heart. She hoped it wasn't too late. The Doctors and nurses relaxed, and she could tell that he was out of immediate danger.

"How is he?" Karishma asked as soon as the ER nurse came out.

"He is stable now." She replied, apparently recognizing Karishma as a fellow nurse.

"How serious was it?" Karishma inquired further.

"We got to him pretty quick. He isn't out of the woods but looks like he will make it through. We had two emergency contacts you and his daughter. Lucky you got here so fast." The nurse skimmed the chart then left Karishma staring at Raj through the glass.

Karishma never knew Raj had a daughter. He had mentioned he had some serious relationships in the past but just that nothing had really worked out. The exhaustion caught up with her as she slumped into the chair just outside Raj's room.

***

Karishma woke to the sound of hurried footsteps. She saw a girl in her early twenties looking in at Raj.
The girl noticed Karishma and asked, "Are you here with my father?"

"Yes, I'm his friend."

"I'm Nikita. He looks terrible. It's been so long since I have seen him. Will he be ok?" Nikita asked.
Karishma hugged Nikita and she graciously accepted it. They were both worried about Raj. Karishma checked her watch and realized how late it was and how little sleep she had. She took Nikita into Raj's room. He looked so peaceful asleep. As much as Karishma wanted to stay to make sure he was recovering well, she needed to rest. Plus, now his daughter was there to help look after him.

Her dreams that night were fitful. Sometimes there were about amazing moments with Rakesh, sometimes about Raj in pain on the ground and sometimes it was Varun's hipster beard. She wished he would just disappear from her memory. He was gone forever from her life, but he still wouldn't leave her alone.

***

She arrived at the hospital earlier than usual to check on Raj. He had been moved to recovery and was awake. She found him talking excitedly with Nikita and they were both laughing a lot.

"Karishma! good to see you. This is my daughter, Nikita," Raj proudly stated as she walked in.

"We met yesterday. How are you feeling?" Karishma asked.

"Like I got hit by a bus, but it got Nikita near me. I can't believe how big she is now," he said.

"Yes Pap, I'm not a kid anymore. It's been way too long," Nikita said holding his hand.

Karishma was happy to see them reunited. It looked like they had a lot to catch up on, and Raj looked so happy to have family around. Karishma didn't really have any family; only child, deadbeat dad and she and her mom hadn't talked in ages. Maybe that's why Rakesh feels so special to her. He already feels so comfortable, like family.

Doctor Patwari stopped her in the hall on the way to her department.

"You're in early today." he said.

"I have a friend in the emergency room. Was just checking on him," she answered.

"Good news, from today, since your main patient is gone, you will be back on normal rotation. Just like you wanted," he said with his eyes lurking on her cleavage.

"What do you mean? He's gone?" Karishma couldn't believe it.

"Mr. Anand was discharged last night. Now back to work. Chop chop." Patwari told her turning around and leaving her alone.

Karishma felt like a bolt of lightning hit her. "He was discharged? Did he leave a message for me?" She wanted to ask these questions, but she knew she couldn't ask them to Doctor Patwari. Confused and jumbled, she felt lost. She went to the reception to see if Saranya knew something.

"Hey, Saranya." she said trying to sound calm and casually.

"Oh, hey, Karishma." The beautiful reception girl replied with her cute Thai accent.

"So, the patient in room 23B got discharged?" Karishma knew that if Saranya knew something, she would tell her. She was the queen of hospital gossip.

"Oh yeah. That was your patient, right. He left in a strange way." She reminisced.

"What was strange?" Karishma pretended that she was in the gossip mood.

"His wife came to visit, and we could hear her yelling all the way down the hall. She practically dragged him out of the ward." Saranya continued. "She looked super pissed."

"And?" Karishma was confused enough already and this just added to the mystery.

"And nothing. She just did the paperwork, and off they went." Saranya continued.

"So, the patient didn't say anything." Karishma was curious to death to know if he had left her any message.

"No. He just went with her without even saying goodbye or thank you. You should ask Navjot, she was on duty with him when his loud wife came. Sorry darling need to answer that." Saranya picked up the ringing phone…

Karishma rushed to Rakesh's room hoping he had left her something. The room was already completely clean. As she was leaving she saw Navjot.

"Navjot, was there anything left in room 23B? A note or message?" she sounded desperate.

Navjot gave her a strange look, "No, no notes or anything. Just his wife came and got all angry. Yelling at him, yelling at the nurses." She grinned saying this.

"You're sure he didn't leave me a message?" Karishma pleaded.

"No. why would he?" Navjot seemed offended, but Karishma didn't give her reaction a second thought.

Despite hours of searching, Karishma couldn't find anything. He was just gone. She guessed that maybe he tried to leave a message, but he couldn't because the wife was there. Why was his wife so angry if they were barely together? Maybe she was really an awful woman and that's why Rakesh turned to her? Her heart ached for him. They finally connected and then he was cruelly taken away from her. She knew she could find his data in the computer system, but she would have to fill the papers and they would ask so many unnecessary questions. She had to find a way.

Chapter 8

It had been a week since Rakesh was discharged and still no word from him. Karishma couldn't help but think about him and wonder where he was. She anxiously waited for him to come see her or call. Every day she would get up and get ready, hoping that Rakesh would show up in the hospital and swoop her off her feet. And every day she would come back saddened and hurt. She replayed the night they made love in her head over and over again.

She was having trouble focusing on her job. Karishma always loved nursing, but now she was just going through the motions. The only thing that excited her was the chance to get into the reception computer and get Rakesh's info without having to tell anyone about it. She spent all her free time after work googling him and looking for any traces of him on social media. She even found some articles about his company and tried calling with a fake name, but she couldn't get through. All she needed was one moment when Saranya was away from her desk for some gossip session. She only needed a few minutes with her computer unattended. Karishma was getting desperate.

Vinita didn't seem offended anymore and slowly started to talk to Karishma again. Karishma watched her flirting again with the cafeteria manager when her phone vibrated. It was a message from an unknown number.

"Hello, beautiful. Did you miss me?" The text read. Karishma's heart started beating faster as she knew that was the message she waited for. She could hardly breathe. He had messaged her first. This was even better than she had hoped for.
"Rakesh?" Karishma replied hurriedly. It was hard to wait for a reply.

"Wow. You were expecting my text, weren't you?" She read the next message.

Karishma let out a giggle of happiness.

"I can't stop thinking about that night. Then you left without saying goodbye or anything," Karishma replied without thinking.

She was counting seconds for him to reply but the message came a few hours later.

"Oh, I'm sorry, sweetheart." She read. "I'll explain everything to you when I see you." Karishma's stomach filled with butterflies when she read, "When I see you."

"So, he is planning on seeing me." Karishma thought. She decided to call him. She needed to hear his voice, but he declined the request after just a single ring.

"Don't call. Just text. I will send you an address. Meet me there."

"Okay. I'm excited my dear," Karishma texted back immediately.

"9765 Anitha Way, Apartment #16. 9 PM. Today" Karishma looked up the address on Google Maps. It was far outside of town, but it didn't matter. She would go anywhere, anytime to see him again.

She rushed home to prepare. She decided to go all out with full makeup, fancy shoes, earrings, and a little black dress. After dressing up, she looked in the mirror and barely recognized herself. She was so used to seeing herself in nurse scrubs, that she forgot how good she looked when she dressed up. She couldn't wait to show Rakesh.

She grabbed a taxi and arrived a few minutes before 9. It was an old but well-kept building at the end of a sleepy cul-de-sac. Karishma found the apartment, knocked on the door and waited anxiously. It was a normal, nondescript door, but Karishma felt like she was standing at the entrance to the royal palace where she will finally be reunited with her prince.

"Who is it?" She recognized Rakesh's voice.

"Karishma." Her voice trembled.

Rakesh opened the door and pulled her inside quickly. Karishma hugged Rakesh and tried to kiss him but he was too busy glancing worriedly down the hallway.

"Did anybody see you?" Rakesh asked.

She was confused but she replied, "No, I don't think so." She was too happy to worry about his interrogative questions.

As soon as the door shut they began to passionately kiss. The apartment was bigger than it looked but reasonably sparse. It looked barely lived in. Rakesh steered her towards the bedroom There was only a big old wooden bed in the room. She sat on the bed.

Rakesh grabbed a glass of whisky. "Would you like some?" he asked Karishma, handing her glass.

"What is it?" Karishma asked.

"It's Rampur Single Malt, my favorite," Rakesh said, taking a sip of his glass. "I really missed it in the hospital."

Karishma giggled and leaned over to kiss Rakesh, but Rakesh stopped her by putting his finger on her lips.

"Karishi, if we are going to do this." Rakesh started. "We need to lay down some rules. You can't tell anyone. No one can know about us. Never take the same taxi or let anyone follow you. The more careful you are the better."

She was a bit surprised by Rakesh's approach but at this moment she missed his body so much that she didn't really care about any rules, she would accept them all.

"You know, because of the kids." he added awkwardly. "You can't call my cell. If you want to talk, just send me a text. And if I don't reply, don't text me back. I will get back to you when I can."

"I don't understand. Why?" Karishma asked with the last resort of a free will that she knew she would lose immediately if he kissed her.

"Because I said so," Rakesh declared. "You can only come here when I tell you." He added further with a stronger voice.

She felt like crying and looked at him sadly. One thought crossed through her mind like an arrow "What if this is a mistake?" She wondered if he was just another Varun trying to use her.

But then she saw his face soften, "Listen, I know it is a lot, but I have to protect my kids. I also want to protect you from people's gossip. I want you. If it wasn't for the children I would be all yours." He caressed her hand while saying this.

"Okay, as you say," Karishma gave up. Although she didn't like any of this secrecy, she wasn't about to leave. She had missed him so much and she felt that things would change over time.

Rakesh sipped the last drop of his whisky, put the glass aside, and pulled Karishma closer for a kiss. She willingly leaned against him and put her hand on his thigh. She loved the feeling of his tongue invading her mouth, his juicy lips against hers. Rakesh kissed her with a hunger that made Karishma realize he missed her as much as she missed him. Rakesh put his hand on her thigh and rubbed it, leaving her moaning. She bit his lower lip slowly while Rakesh squeezed her harder. Rakesh worked his way through her dress to reach her already wet vagina.

He started rubbing her from over her panties. "Oh, baby, you are so wet down there." he gasped.

"I am wet for you, Rakesh." she replied.

Rakesh slowly put his fingers inside her panties and pushed them into her opening. Karishma loved the way his fingers felt inside of her. Rakesh started slowly moving his finger in and out of her while rubbing her clit. Karishma bit her lip to keep from howling. She started rubbing Rakesh's cock from over his pants. She could feel him growing harder in her hand.

She undid his belt and slid his trousers down. Her hand wrapped around his raised shaft. She started rubbing it while Rakesh was fingering her fervently. "Let me taste it." Karishma managed to tell him in between heavy breaths.

Rakesh stood and presented his rock-hard penis. She smiled at him, then grabbed his cock. She started with a couple of steady strokes then licked his lengthy penis from base to tip. She kissed the tip of it and slid her mouth around it. Rakesh looked at the ceiling, moaning with pleasure. Karishma tried to take as much of him in her mouth as she could without gagging. She sucked on his cock, bobbing her head to and fro, making a slurping sound. It was Karishma's first time enjoying a blowjob so much - she did it with other men, but not because she wanted to, because she felt obligated to. She loved Rakesh's penis, and she loved the feeling of it against the back of her throat. Karishma held its head inside her mouth while stroking the shaft rapidly. She then tried to put all of it inside her mouth again but failed. "Needs practice." she thought.

After a few minutes of oral pleasure, Rakesh asked her to lay on the bed. Karishma slid out of her dress and quickly removed her panties. Rakesh ripped off his shirt and climbed on top of her. As he kissed her, she felt his penis rubbing against the outside of her vagina. Rakesh gently slid the tip of his cock inside of her and then, with a single hard thrust, put all of his length inside of her. Karishma gasped with pleasure. Rakesh started moving in and out of her giving her joy and delight with every movement. She grabbed Rakesh's firm buttocks and pulled him even harder towards her with every hump. He grabbed Karishma's breast and tickled her nipple. After a few more minutes of Rakesh thrusting on top of Karishma, he rolled onto his back and asked her to get on top of him. It was Karishma's turn to ride. She got up and placed her wet vagina on top of Rakesh's cock and sat on it, taking his dick inside of her. She put her hands on his shoulder and started moving up and down on his cock. She loved having Rakesh inside of her. She loved the touch of his body against hers and the feeling of his huge penis expanding her tight pussy. Karishma started moving fast as she felt her orgasm building.

"I am about to cum, Rakesh." she moaned in pleasure.

"Cum for me, baby." he encouraged her pushing his dick even stronger into her.

Karishma put her head on Rakesh's chest, closed her eyes, and started slamming her body down onto his penis as quickly as she could. The pressure was building inside her so much she could barely hold it. Then just as it released, and the warm feeling spread through her body, she felt him ejaculate inside of her. Feeling of his hot love juice inside her vagina was too much for Karishma, she came hard and loud. Her whole body was trembling when she finished off with Rakesh inside of her. She stayed in the same position for a few moments.

They laid together for a moment, then Rakesh got up and gruffly said, "C'mon, let's go. It's late." Karishma felt a little change in his tone but ignored it. She just wanted this moment with him to last as long as possible.

"Can't we just stay a little longer?" she asked childishly.

"No, Karishi, I need to go home." He said pushing gently Karishma aside and standing up.

"Okay." she said, making a sad face. "Will you drop me off?"

Rakesh's eyes flashed with well-hidden irritation, "I told you the rules. If you want to keep doing this, you need to follow them. I will call you and pay for a cab." he said, pulling up his pants. "I can't let anyone see you with me." he added more softly.

Karishma had never seen the angry side of Rakesh before. She was a little bit scared, but also a little bit turned on. She liked that he was ordering her around a bit. She had always liked a bad boy... to a point.

Rakesh left. Karishma laid on the bed, still naked. She had mixed feelings about all of this. He was so hot taking control and having his way with her. He was simply irresistible, but there was also an edge that scared her a bit. She wanted to stop herself before she went too far down this path, but she couldn't. Rakesh captured her with his personality and charm. Karishma realized that she loved him. She had fallen in love with him the first time she saw him.

"Wasn't he a bit strange today?" there was always a part of Karishma's mind which was against all of it and questioned her affection. Karishma tried to push this voice to the back of her mind but she couldn't completely ignore it. "He called you, he had sex with you and left. Isn't it obvious what he wanted from you?", the annoying voice was trying to annoy her again.

Karishma got to taxi and went back to her place. She grabbed dinner from Raj's and went to her apartment to get some rest.

Chapter 9

It was a new routine for Karishma - wake up early, go to work, come back home, wait desperately for his text. When she got lucky, she would go to their secret place, have a glass of Rampur Single Malt and end up having an amazing sex with the multiply orgasm guaranteed. She could call her week a good one when she saw Rakesh three times during any seven days. With regular meetings their sex just got better and better. She also trusted him more, as he was always charming and sweet, just as in the beginning. Karishma noticed that to keep him stay this way, all she had to do was to obey his few simple rules - make sure no one was seeing her walking into the apartment, not to call him, not talk about him in the hospital or with her friends. The more she knew the rules and she followed them, the happier he was, and all Karishma wanted was to make Rakesh happy and satisfied with her.

From time to time Karishma felt guilty that sometimes she wanted more from him. One day she asked him to do something other than sex. She begged him to take her out for a dinner, so they could just talk and get know each other better than just through sex. She wanted to know about him, about his kids, about his job or just about anything. Rakesh agreed to it after a struggle, but in the end, he cooked dinner in the apartment and it quickly just turned into traditional sex session. Rakesh was good at seducing and Karishma was too weak to resist his charm and strong personality.

One day she dared to ask him why they only had sex.

"I can't resist you, babe, that's the best sex ever." he replied making her happy and sad at the same time.
The part of Karishma, that didn't like this relationship, was convinced that he only wants sex. Georgette focused on the good things and tried her to best to silence the doubting voice, with the time passing by she became exceptionally good at this.

***

One day her doubts were stronger than usual – the sex was incredible but just she needed more. Karishma was lying on the bed still breathing heavily from a long session. She watched Rakesh getting dressed, she glanced at his empty whisky glass. Unexpectedly she felt this glass - she served her purpose and then was left on the side table.

"Is this going anywhere? How long are we going to keep just fucking?" she suddenly said to him.

"What?" Rakesh asked her with his mind occupied by something or someone else.

"I want something more than this," she said surprisingly even to herself.

"What do you mean by that, Karishma?" Rakesh asked, looking in her eyes for the first time since they had sex.

"I mean, I don't want to do it like this anymore. I want to enjoy our relationship like every other couple. I don't want to sneak around like some sort of cheap whore." Karishma didn't know where these words were coming from, she seemed to be surprised with them as much as Rakesh was.

"I thought we understood each other. This is great, but I have a family and can't just give that up. Don't you like being with me here? Having me?" his voice was smoothing, and his hand gently touched her hand.
"I do. I love seeing you, spending time with you, having sex with you. I love all of it," Karishma said. "But it isn't just about sex. I want to be your partner. You told me that you and your wife are only together for the kids and that you always fight, so why do that at all. They will be ok."

"It's not that easy," Rakesh said slowly and stopped touching her hand.

"Why?" she quietly asked although she knew the answer.

"Because it's not. I need more time to clean this up. Now I have to go." Rakesh said with frustration.

"Why can't it be something more. I thought you loved me?" Karishma didn't give up.

"Why can't you be happy with what we have? Why do you have to ask for more?" Rakesh's tone was intensifying with every word he spoke. He didn't expect this type of conversation and it visibly made him annoyed.

Karishma was scared by this aggressive tone. She didn't say anything and just looked at the floor. Rakesh realized he had frightened Karishma, so he came near her and hugged her.

"Listen, baby, I didn't mean to raise my voice. It's just that I have so much in my mind. I am going on a business trip to France, and when I come back, we'll talk about this." he said with a caring and cautious tone.

"Okay, when?" Karishma smiled and started to get ready to leave.

"In a week or so. I will text you when I get back. Don't call or text first. I will be in touch." And he left.

***

Karishma got dropped off in front of her apartment late at night and saw the light in Raj's restaurant. She thought it was too late for him to be open and sudden fear that something had happened to him speared her heart. She went into the shop and started to look for him, but she couldn't find him anywhere. Karishma called out, but no one answered. She worried that he had another heart attack and was lying unconscious somewhere in the kitchen. She looked behind the counters but couldn't see him.

"He must be in that room." Karishma thought, looking at the back office. Just outside the door, she finally heard some noises. She peeped into the room and saw Raj. Raj was better than ok, as he was having sex with a woman quite younger than him...The same woman she saw another day leaving his restaurant.

The young lady was lying on her back, and Raj was pushing his penis inside of her, his body was covered with sweat and the woman was moaning in pleasure. Karishma stifled a laugh at the image of Raj's big belly flopping around but then noticed he had a very impressive size of penis, just as expected from a Punjabi man. It looked like a huge brown eggplant with decent size balls at the end. His partner was a petit woman and it looked like this enormous dick could make her harm. However, the girl was moaning with pleasure, pushing herself even more onto Raj's tool. Karishma coughed out a laugh thinking how lucky this woman was. She got a bit excited herself watching this big dick pounding this little woman.

The humped girl looked towards the door and freaked out after finding Karishma looking at them. She screamed, and Raj jumped grabbing a kitchen towel to cover himself up.

"Oh, Crap, Karishma." Raj shouted. "What are you doing here?", his gigantic penis was sticking out from the towel.

"I saw the light on, I'm sorry but I thought something bad happened to you." Karishma said with a giggle. "I really wasn't trying to snoop, I just thought…. something bad happened." She blushed trying to explain slowly backing out of the room

"No worries dear. Trying to keep my heart strong," he joked with a wink when Karishma was closing the door. She heard the laugh on the other side of the door and a moment later they seemed to go back to what was interrupted.

"It was a good day," thought Karishma lying in her bed. She was glad that Raj seemed healthier than she expected, and, most of all, Rakesh would come back in a week, so they could figure out everything. "Figure out how to live happily ever after together," she thought while falling asleep and dreaming about the floppy belly of Raj, big engagement ring from Rakesh and sucking Vinita's brown nipples.

Chapter 10

Karishma had a fitful week waiting for Rakesh to come back.

She tried to keep her mind off it with work and lots of taco filled visits at Raj's. She even met up with some old friends she hadn't seen in months, but her mind was always drifting to Rakesh and their future together. He should come back any day and it was all she could think about.

"He will be back today." she thought to herself. "We will talk soon and sort things out." Karishma was excited and could not think about anything else.

"Hello, I have been asking for cup of tea. It's almost 5 o'clock!" An old lady Karishma that was taking care of in the hospital said noisily.

"Shit, I forgot again." Karishma thought. She poured a glass of water and gave it to the old lady. "Here you go, Mrs. Patel." she said to the grumpy old English woman, who seemed to always complain.

"Finally!" Mrs. Patel said, taking the cup of Karishma's hand and mumbling some unpleasant comments.

"Kari, Patwari wants to see you in his office." Voice of Vinita came from behind.

"Do you need anything else, Mrs. Patel?" Karishma asked the old lady as politely as she could.
"Like you are of any good." The grumpy lady said with a dissatisfied grimace on her face.

Ignoring her last comment, Karishma went straight to Doctor Patwari's office.

"Karishma I got another complaint about you from a patient." Patwari stated, "I am not sure what happened to you? This says you are not concentrating on your job, ignoring patients, forgetting things. This is not acceptable." Patwari added.

"I am sorry, Doctor Patwari, it won't happen again," Karishma said thinking if that was Mrs. Patel who had complained about her.

"That's what you said last time," Doctor Patwari said. "You were an exemplary nurse here for years. I'm hoping this is the end of it or your days at this hospital are numbered."

"I will sort it out today, Doctor," Karishma said, thinking of Rakesh.

She always prided herself on being good at her job. She graduated top of her class at the nursing school and even when things were going badly with Varun, she always put her job first. What happened to her? Did Rakesh have that big of an effect on her or was it something else? She had to sort things out with him, and fast, or she was out of a job.

***

Day after day passed with no message from Rakesh. She was trying to focus on her job and just work but it was getting harder and harder, every day it was more difficult to find an excuse why he hadn't yet contacted her. She wasn't sleeping well and when she finally managed to fall asleep, she had nightmares with Varun, Rakesh and even Doctor Patwari. When she couldn't sleep, she killed the time spending hours on googling about Rakesh. She could recite all the articles mentioning his company by heart.

After two weeks, when she ran out of potential explanations why he hadn't called yet, she finally reached out.

"Rakesh? Are you there?" she sent a message. Karishma knew he would be mad that she broke a rule and messaged him first, but this was getting ridiculous for her. She needed an answer.

***

Karishma waited for a reply in anguish. She was sitting in the staff room alone, praying that Rakesh would reply.

Saranya from the front desk interrupted her thoughts. "Karishma, I need to step out for a moment. If you aren't busy can you watch reception for me?".

Karishma willingly agreed, sat down at reception and stared at the computer. She knew all the information she craved on Rakesh was hidden there, but if she was caught it would cost her a job and probably her nursing license. She looked around and saw reception was empty, with the heart racing and sweaty palms she double-clicked on the folder of patients' records.

Karishma scrolled through until she found the name "Anand, Rakesh." And hesitated for a moment. She knew it was wrong, but sometimes you must do something extreme to make things right. And, after all, she did much worse things in her life before. And this was just a piece of information. Karishma opened his file, scanned all the info and saw a different phone number than the one she had from him. She also found his home address – he lived in an affluent suburb at least a 45-minute drive away from their secret apartment. She took a quick picture of the file with her mobile, closed the computer and calmly waited for Saranya to came back.

Karishma got angry that he didn't keep his promise to contact her, so she was thinking about going to his house and checking on him discreetly. In the middle of her planning what to tell the wife or children in case they would see her, her cell phone alerted for a notification. She grabbed the phone hurriedly and saw Rakesh's reply.

"I told you not to text." Karishma felt relieved and angry at the same time reading Rakesh's words.

"We were supposed to have a serious conversation. You said were back after a week." She texted back immediately.

"Yeah, I got back a week ago," Rakesh replied. Karishma felt like someone hit her on her face. Rakesh got back from his trip but didn't tell her?

"What? Did you get back a week ago? Why didn't you tell me?" Karishma replied wishing that she could show her anger in her message.

"Been busy," Rakesh replied laconically.

"You could have at least told me that you are back." She texted. "I miss you, and we need to talk about us."

She didn't like being ignored and needed to know why he was treating her like this. She saw that he read the message, but he didn't respond.

After one hour with no response, she texted him again, "when are we going to meet?"

"Not now. Wait for me to message you." He replied after another hour.

Karishma felt frustrated. "Is he losing interest in me?" she was deliberating when thousands of different scenarios were crossing her mind.

"Rakesh, you promised that we will talk about our situation once you get back." She wrote back again almost immediately. "This situation that I don't want to keep this a secret anymore. I want to see you whenever I want and call you whenever I want. And you promised that we would talk about this." She texted again not even waiting for his response. "I want a better relationship. With no boundaries and rules." Karishma kept writing, reaching the point when she could not stop sounding desperate. She stared at the phone waiting for a response.

"I am tired, I am going to sleep. Maybe I will message you later." he texted back.

Karishma was furious. "Maybe he will message me," She thought. "Maybe isn't good enough and he promised we would talk." She felt strong anger rising from deep inside her. After all that time, she deserved answers. She desperately wanted to see him and her mind raced, "I should just show up at his house. If he is messaging me, it means his family is out. No one will know and when he sees me, he will remember why he loves me."

She was slowly convincing herself. She made up her mind, called herself an Uber and headed towards Rakesh's house. She messaged him from the cab, "Is now a good time to talk? Is your wife gone?" Again, she got a read receipt and no answer. She knew he was avoiding her and this made her even more resolute in confronting him.

The cab dropped her in the posh area of town with luxurious houses all around. The driver pulled up in front of a very large residence with a beautifully manicured lawn. She could see a fancy two-seater car and a family minivan in the driveway. When the cab drove away, Karishma hid behind a tree across the street. She waited there for around 15 minutes, staring at the residence's gate. She didn't know what to do, she had planned just to come and surprise him but now it wasn't feeling right. Deliberating whether to call a cab and go back, she saw a beautiful woman coming out of the house with two adorable children in tow. The lady was smiling, and her children were laughing and seemed so happy. Suddenly, Karishma got this vision of the perfect family in the suburbs. She immediately felt both jealous and guilty. She wanted to take the wife's place, wanted those kids to be hers. And Rakesh's.

She watched the minivan with the kids and wife drive away, then waited another ten minutes just to make sure they were not coming back. When she was getting ready to knock on the doors, her phone buzzed.

Rakesh was texting her. "We can meet in an hour, but I don't want to talk. I just want to see you. We can discuss things later, let's just have some fun."

For a moment she hesitated, but then she thought about Raj talking about how things turned around once he went for what he wanted instead of waiting for it. Karishma was sure if she went to meet Rakesh at that apartment then nothing would be different. If she wouldn't take charge, then nothing would ever change. She cautiously walked up to his front door and rang the bell.

Rakesh opened the door finding Karishma standing there with a giant smile on her face. He looked stunned for a minute with his eyes opened wide. Like he didn't believe that she is there.

"Surprise," Karishma said with a gratified smile.

"Are you out of your fucking mind?" Rakesh said furiously, grabbing her hand and pulling inside of the house. "What, are you crazy?" He yelled with red face.

"Aren't you happy to see me?" Karishma said, maintaining a smile on her face, despite the fact her arm was hurting because of his strong grip.

"Happy? Do you know what would have happened if my wife had seen you? How do you even know where I live?" Rakesh was furious and confused.
"I was careful. Don't worry. I just had to see you. We have to talk." Karishma said.

"You are a psychopath," Rakesh said her through his teeth.

His anger made him seem so manly and protective, but this time she was in control and it turned her on.

"I know you are happy to see me." Karishma said, getting near him, "Tell me you didn't miss me?" she asked moving closer to kiss him.

"Karishma, you have to go." He said, stopping her from kissing him.

"Why? You don't want me?" Karishma sounded desperate even to herself.
"This is not how this works," Rakesh said, trying to contain his anger.

"No, I want you to have me right here. I know you missed me. And I missed you too, Rakesh." She said seductively, trying to kiss him again. Karishma felt that once he would sex with her, Rakesh would understand that it's not a bad idea to give their relationship a bit of freedom.

She grabbed Rakesh's hands and kissed him on his lips. Rakesh pushed her backward. Then he grabbed her hand and pulled her towards the bedroom. He threw her on the bed and started undressing. She had never seen Rakesh this aggressive. His temper scared her a bit, but at the same time it made her more turned on. At least she was having him again. Rakesh looked almost like he was glaring as he approached the bed. She leaned towards him for a kiss, but he grabbed her arm and flipped her over.

"Rakesh, you are hurting me," she yelled in surprise.

He ignored her. He pulled her dress up and ripped her panties down harshly. He thrust himself into her roughly. Karishma screamed with pain and surprise. Rakesh put his hand on her mouth and started pounding her from behind. Karishma tried to move, but Rakesh's weight was too much for her. Rakesh was humping her like a jackhammer against concrete. Karishma felt attacked, but her body was still accepting him with a sort of weird pleasure. Her vagina was wet, and her nipples were getting hard. Karishma tried to get in a more comfortable position so it would hurt less. She arched her back and got her knees underneath her, spreading her legs and Rakesh took her doggy-style. If this was how he got out his frustration, then fine. At least she was his again.

Rakesh spit on his dick and said, "This is what you want, huh?" He then rammed his dick into her ass.

Karishma felt a jolt of pain as he shoved the full length of his penis into her asshole. She had tried anal sex before with Varun, but she never liked it much and they used lube and took it slowly. Even then it was painful, and this felt even worse. All the pleasure was gone and there was just pain.

She put her face on a pillow and screamed into it, as Rakesh was pushing his cock in and out of her. Karishma didn't feel special anymore. For the first time, she realized that Rakesh wasn't making love with her instead, he was just fucking her. The electric feeling of his touch was gone. She wanted to be his partner and to love him but all she felt from him now was cruelty. Karishma was squeezing the sheets on the bed, waiting for him to finish. After a few more agonizing minutes, Rakesh grabbed her hips and started pumping even faster. She could tell he was about to come. He pushed his entire shaft inside her and grunted as he reached his climax. Karishma could feel ropes of hot semen inside of her as Rakesh finished off in her ass.

Rakesh pulled out of her butt and started to dress again. Karishma couldn't say anything - she was too shocked of what had just happened, wanted him to smile at her, kiss her, do anything to make her feel special and not like a cheap whore. She got up and stood there, waiting for Rakesh to say something. Drops of Rakesh's cum were dripping down her thigh.

"Go get dressed, I will drop you off," Rakesh said coldly without even looking at her.

Karishma didn't say anything, she just went into the washroom. "He just raped you." The voice said in her head.

"No, he didn't." another voice tried to deny.

"He did, he used you." first voice spoke again.

"He was just frustrated. You broke his rules and pushed too much. You wanted this as much as he did. Now he is going to drop you off. He never did this before." She reassured herself.

Karishma cleaned herself and washed her face. She was about to go out of the washroom when she heard a woman's voice and a commotion in the bedroom.

"Every time they cancel on us." the female voice said.

"It's rude of them, I know. But you can't stress yourself on it right, Prakriti?" Rakesh sounded nervously.

Karishma hid behind the shower curtain. For a moment she thought about confronting them but then she realized it would kill completely any chance she had with Rakesh.

"It's just annoying. I mean who does that? But I left the kids at their friends' house, so we have some time alone," Prakriti said seductively. Karishma thought it sounded like they weren't in that bad of a relationship after all.

"What is this? This isn't mine" Prakriti suddenly sounded angry.

"I would never wear an earring like this. Whose is this Rakesh?" Karishma reached up to her ear and realized one of her earrings had fallen off during the sex.

"I don't know," Rakesh said. "I'm not in charge of the earrings."

"You expect me to believe that some random earring just shows up on my bed when I'm not here? Is it that slut nurse from the hospital?" She asked. "I knew exactly was going on between you two."

Karishma froze hearing this "Does she know about me?". Her mind raced, "I was so careful, how this is possible?"

"C'mon babe. You know there was no one else here. It's probably from one of the cleaning ladies? It is not the first time when you accuse me of something without good reason." Rakesh was grasping at straws but still sounded surprisingly confident.

"You are so full of it," Prakriti said with much less anger in her voice. Surprisingly Rakesh's explanations were convincing enough for her.

"I think you are just annoyed that your friends ditched you. We have a night without the kids for once, let's make the most of it." Rakesh said smoothly.

"I swear to God Rakesh, if you are screwing around..." Prakriti started.

"Baby, you need to relax. Let's grab a bite. I'll take you to that Italian place you love." Rakesh cut her off.

Karishma heard the voices getting quieter as they left the room. Her heart was pounding, and she felt like she should just run, but then Rakesh opened the bathroom door. He was furious. His eyes were blazing like a bonfire and his face turned red.

"Get the fuck out of here." He said in a low but harsh tone. "And don't you dare try this shit again. Or you will regret it."

Karishma couldn't say anything. Rakesh pulled his keys out of his pocket and yelled to Prakriti that he found them. Then he gave one last angry glare to Karishma before walking away.

Karishma was scared and speechless, she waited for a minute or two before coming out of the bathroom. She went slowly towards the window and looked out to see Rakesh and Prakriti driving away. She took one last look around the room to make sure she didn't leave anything else behind, then walked down the stairs. At the front door, she turned around and looked at the perfect house that she so desperately wanted to be hers and the life with Rakesh she wanted so badly. She started to cry. The dream was over.

Chapter 11

Days passed since the catastrophic night at Rakesh's house. The night had left Karishma so confused, hurt and lost. She still cared for Rakesh and thought back on how special he made her feel, but she couldn't forget his terrible temper. Then Karishma thought about Prakriti, the poor wife of Rakesh. Prakriti didn't seem bad at all, just a normal wife whose husband cheats on her. Rakesh had hurt her physically and emotionally, even more than Varun had, but for some reason Karishma still wanted to forgive him.

The original plan was to keep things casual and not let it get too far too fast. She wondered where it went wrong and if it was possible to go back. Even after their fights and that terrible night, she wanted to go back to spending evenings with him at his little apartment, drinking whisky and getting lost in each other. Karishma pushed too hard to get more, but she thought he still cared. He would call. He had to. Rakesh would forgive her.

In the meantime, Karishma refocused on life at the hospital. Doctor Patwari had been keeping a close eye on her and she didn't want to let him down. To keep from thinking about Rakesh she started leaving her phone in her locker at work and trying to just be in the moment.

At the hospital Karishma was assigned to an odd new patient. He was an old grey hair man, that the hospital staff called "Baba", and all the nurses were asking him to tell what is written in the stars for them. Vinita told Karishma that he could see the future and for Vinita it was full of great fun and many men. Karishma thought that anyone who spent five minutes with Vinita would realize she had a future full of men, but Karishma was still curious and wanted to ask the Baba about her future. Today was his last day in the hospital, so it was the last chance to get a reading.

"Here is your tea, Baba Munjal," Karishma handed him a cup of green tea.

"Thank you, dear." He said in a slow and resonant tone. Baba indeed looked like the man who could have some powers.

"Do you need anything else?" Karishma asked.

"No dear, not me. The question is what you need?" he sounded weird. "I sense a lot of discomfort in you." Karishma couldn't tell if he was actually looking at her or off into space.

"Don't worry sir. I'm fine," Karishma said unconvincingly, thinking how to ask about the prediction about her future with Rakesh.

"Let's see how fine you really are." Baba said, sitting up in his bed. "Come here. Let me have your hands and look into you."

Karishma felt excited. She sat down next to the bed and the man took her hands. He stared deeply into her eyes and she suddenly felt uncomfortable.

"Young lady, you are deep in the turmoil. The turmoil of love," he stated with a confident tone.

"Not bad," she thought, "but what single girl in Mumbai isn't in the turmoil of love?"

Baba Munjal continued looking into her hand. "You found love in the past, but..." his voice suddenly trembled a bit and trailed off. He stared with panicked eyes, like he just saw a ghost.

Karishma demanded, "I want to know about love now, not in the past. Please tell me about the future!"
He kept glancing from her eyes to her hand, mumbling something indistinctly that sounded like a prayer that she couldn't understand.

"The past always comes back to us. And your past is your future," he said switching back to English and immediately pushed her hands away. Baba looked like he saw something in her that scared him to death.

"What does the future hold?" Karishma kept asking, trying to find out what he had seen that could possibly be so bad. "Please tell me Baba" she begged nervously.

"Leave me now. Leave me immediately and don't come here again!" he screamed, "You are the devil, leave me now!" his eyes were red and full of fear. He avoided looking at her while his body was trembling with shivers. Karishma stared in shock at his outburst.

"But Baba Munjal..." she tried to calm him down, but he was sitting there with closed eyes, shaking and saying words in a foreign language. Karishma ran from the room with tears in her eyes, not understanding why he thought she was the devil. "Did he see Prakriti and thought I destroyed her marriage?" She wondered. Karishma was left sad and even more scared and concerned.

***

Karishma finally heard from Rakesh. She was so ecstatic to see his name pop up on her phone that she would have gone anywhere just to see him and apologize. Rakesh wanted to meet with her. It looked like a good sign.

Karishma arrived at the apartment at the exact time and knocked on the door. She heard footsteps approaching. Rakesh opened the door and went back in without saying a word. Karishma felt weird but didn't say anything. She went in and closed the door behind her.

"We need to talk," he said abruptly.

"Are you still mad at me?" Karishma asked.

"Of course I am. You show up at my house and almost get caught by my wife. What were you thinking? I could have lost everything," Rakesh said furiously.

"I thought things were terrible with your wife, that you were just together for the kids. Then why not start over… with me?" Karishma could see he was still very angry.

"Start over with you? How stupid are you? You're a good lay. That's it." Rakesh's voice got louder with each word.

"So, it was just sex for you?" Karishma couldn't believe it, she felt like someone was choking her. "I thought you loved me."

"Love? When did I say anything about loving you?" He said insultingly.

"Please, Rakesh." Karishma couldn't believe it. She fell to the ground and started crying.

"This was never more than just sex. If you followed the rules and weren't a complete psycho, maybe we could have kept this up, but it looks like you are too stupid for even that." he was yelled her.

Rakesh's anger grew and his words got harsher. Karishma stopped listening as he continued to insult her and talk about how she was nothing to him. Karishma couldn't even respond.

Finally, she found her voice, "Rakesh, I'm sorry. I know I made a mistake going to your house, but I love you. I can't help that. I just want us to be together."

"Get this through your head. We had some fun. It was a good time. That was it. Get over it. Get out of my life." His words cut her soul like knife blades.

Karishma was shocked by everything that was happening. She thought that they would make things right, but they got worse. "I told you that he was the same as Varun." The voice that Karishma suppressed spoke again. "Rakesh wanted to use you like every other man. Actually, he is worse than other men, at least they would disappear after using you, but he came back to use you again and again." Karishma covered her ears to stop the voice. Tears streamed down her face as she began to sob uncontrollably.

"Stop crying, you look even uglier than usual when you cry," he spat the words at her, "I'm leaving Karishma. It's over. Goodbye." Rakesh walked out of the apartment and left Karishma sitting on the floor crying.

This wasn't the man that Karishma loved. This was someone else that she didn't know at all. The Rakesh she loved was a caring and loving gentleman. Karishma heard words she never expected from him. She was so naive, she thought this was real love. She thought she had found the perfect man and that it would work between them despite his wife and children. "A person must always fight for love," she reminded herself what Raj was always saying.

Karishma woke up on the floor of the apartment thinking it was all just a bad dream. After realizing where she was, Karishma knew it wasn't. Her body ached, and she could barely sit up. After some struggle, she finally managed to get to her feet. It was 5:35 AM. She was supposed to be at work soon for the morning shift, so she called a taxi. She phoned Vinita.

"Hey Kari, you're almost late today. Doctor Patwari is all hot and bothered about it." Vinita started.

"I'm really sick. Fever, aches all of that. Can you tell him for me? If I call him he will just be mad." Karishma lied.
"I got you girl," Vinita hung up.

Karishma got home, crawled into bed and fell asleep with Rakesh's angry words still in her head. Maybe Baba Munjal was right. He saw despair and sadness and that's all she felt now.

***

Karishma thought about Varun. He had toyed with her emotions, but she made him regret it. Rakesh was doing the same to her. Raj was right, she deserved more. Karishma felt like she needed to talk to Raj. He was the only true friend she had. When getting ready to leave she saw an envelope that someone had slipped under her door.

"I can't live like this anymore, please don't cry after me, I hate myself for doing all the bad things to you and I hope one day you will forgive me. You will be happier when I am gone so I don't screw anything else... I'm so sorry, goodbye forever. God and you please forgive me. Rakesh."

Karishma read the letter over and over, trying to understand the words. "It's that easy for him?" she thought. "He insulted me, raped me, called me names, and now says he's sorry? He gives me the brush off like 'it's not you, it's me?'. She took the letter and crumpled it in her hands.

Karishma's sadness turned into a more powerful force; anger. She was mad at Rakesh, but also mad at herself. She needed closure, a better closure than this letter. She was ready to let him go, but she also wanted to have a chance to say a proper good-bye and maybe get one last kiss.

Without thinking, Karishma called a cab to their secret apartment. She knew Rakesh spent quite some time at the apartment after the office. Hopefully he would be there tonight. For the first time she was going there for answers instead of for sex.
Karishma got dropped off a few streets away in order to be more discreet and walked carefully to the building. She suddenly stopped when she saw Navjot, her colleague from the hospital, entering the building. What was another nurse doing here? Karishma's heart started to beat faster as all the pieces of the puzzle began to fall into place. She followed Navjot but kept her distance, watching as Navjot buzzed Rakesh's apartment and then headed down the hall.

"Why is she coming to visit Rakesh?" Karishma wondered but she sort of knew the answer already.

Karishma peeked around the corner and saw Rakesh opening the door and embracing Navjot. Navjot entered the apartment while Rakesh looked around suspiciously. Luckily, Karishma was hidden around the corner.

"Of all people, Navjot!" Karishma thought. If it was Vinita, she wouldn't have been surprised, but Navjot was always quieter and less "friendly." She was very average looking, so why would Rakesh like her?

Karishma imagined herself bursting in through the front door but knew that wasn't realistic. She needed to see what was really going on, so Karishma snuck around the outside of the building. Luckily the apartment was on the ground floor and Karishma just had to climb a small fence to get onto the patio. She remembered looking out the big bay doors onto the patio and wondered if people could see inside. Now she was on the outside looking in and it gave a pretty clear view into the bedroom. Karishma saw Rakesh laying naked on the same bed they shared, with Navjot riding him. Her small tits bounced as she moved herself up and down on his cock. The glass of Rampur Single Malt was on the bedside table.

Karishma was so angry she wanted to scream. "How dare he do this to me? To Prakriti? To his kids? He is just another cheating bastard, even worse than Varun. He is cheating on everyone!" She gritted her teeth as the rage-filled thoughts flooded her mind.

Everything finally started to make sense. She had seen Rakesh flirting with Navjot but ignored it. Karishma remembered Navjot getting weird when she asked her about Rakesh leaving a message. Or the time when angry Prakriti came to pick up Rakesh from the hospital - Prakriti must have seen something between Rakesh and Navjot. That was why he checked out so fast and why Prakriti didn't trust him. Or another day when Karishma was in Rakesh's house - Prakriti asked him about the nurse, but she meant Navjot, not Karishma. The rose-tinted glasses fell from Karishma's eyes and she saw clearly what type of man Rakesh was. But her heart just didn't listen to her mind, "women in love are so blinded" she thought. All she wanted was closure and at least one last moment when their bodies will unite for the last time. Just before Karishma's dreams would vanish forever.

***

"I can't live like this anymore. Please don't cry after me. I hate myself for doing all the bad things to you and I hope one day you will forgive me. You will be happier when I am gone and can't screw anything else up… I'm so sorry, goodbye forever. Rakesh."

Karishma was reading her letter over and over again, crushing the edges of the smushed paper. She was sitting on the big wooden bed in their hidden apartment. Rakesh was in the kitchen getting ready for their final goodbye sex

Rakesh called her, "I finished my whisky, going to have another one. Do you want one?"

"No," Karishma called back. "All I want is you, Rakesh," she thought sadly but didn't say aloud.

Rakesh entered the room with a full glass of whisky and a hungry look in his eye. Karishma quickly hid the letter. He didn't pretend to be a gentleman anymore. He treated her more like a prostitute than a girlfriend. No hugging, no kissing, only dry comments about her look.

"It's been a long day, let me have a quick shower before we get to work," Rakesh said placing the empty whisky glass next to her.

Karishma gestured for him to go ahead. She looked around the apartment. She came here often, but this time was the last. And the last time she would ever see Rakesh. He kept repeating that their secret relationship must end. She was apparently just a short fling, a banter, as he said that day. But finally, she was ready to say goodbye. Karishma would miss the amazing sex and uncontrollable connection, but she was ready. Very ready.

***

A sudden crash in the bathroom and Rakesh's scream brought her back to reality. Karishma looked down at the letter in her hands. She sighed, put the letter carefully on the night table next to the empty glass.

"Finally," Karishma thought. Even though she impatiently waited for this noise, she gave a few more minutes before she decided to open the bathroom door. She knew what she would see and what came next because she had prepared it well, there was no hesitation or possibility that Karishma would miss something. No wonder she passed her nurse exams as the best student in the class. She took one last deep breath and opened the doors.

Rakesh was on the floor holding his throat, a white foam mixed with red blood was dripping from his mouth. He looked at Karishma with begging in his eyes.

Rakesh still apparently didn't understand what had happened and why his lover, the qualified nurse, didn't try to help him. Karishma felt that maybe she owed him an explanation, but after some deliberation, she decided he didn't deserve it. So she simply stood there waiting and looking at him. Rakesh's eyes grew large as he tried to speak but only a gurgle and some foam came out. Rakesh tried to reach her leg, but she moved back.
"He looks much worse dying than Varun did," the voices in Karishma's head finally agreed on something. She remembered that Varun was also quicker to die. It took him only a few seconds, but she tried to make it as quick and painless as possible, paying attention to mixing the medicines in a correct dose. For Rakesh, she didn't care about it, "At least he can feel some pain. It is only fair after all the pain he caused me." Both voices applauded.

"Don't bleed so much please, blood makes you even uglier," Karishma said aloud, remembering the comment Rakesh made about her.

Rakesh looked at her with a surprise, probably finally realizing what was happening. With the last spasm, he tried to reach out and grab Karishma again but was already too weak. Rakesh's eyes rolled back into his head as he violently convulsed. Karishma stepped back and watched his final spasms with peaceful contemplation. Rakesh finally became still. Without wasting precious time, Karishma pulled on the rubber gloves and got down to work.

She took the half-empty aspirin box from her pocket and put it next to his empty whisky glass. Karishma was finally at peace - she still had so much to live for and her life was not ending with Rakesh, Varun or any other guy. She had a job that she loved and she was really good at it. Karishma was an amazing nurse. Only a good nurse like herself always remembers patients' habits, like a glass of Rampur Single Malt before sex.

"Yes, it was good to be a nurse and it was even better to have access to all the patients' charts in the hospital. Karishma remembered from the very first day she read his chart that Rakesh was severely allergic to aspirin. His overly cautious rules were now working in her favor. No one knew they were together or ever saw her with him. Last but certainly not least, it was good to have a letter from him that made a perfect suicide note.

Karishma walked through the apartment making sure she hadn't left anything behind. She went through his trousers and found two phones inside. One was an old flip phone and the other fancy smartphone with his wife and kids for a background. Karishma took the flip phone and meticulously deleted all messages related to her. She left all Navjot's messages, just in case some nosy detective got suspicious. She thoroughly cleaned the apartment to get rid of all her fingerprints and looked at Rakesh's corpse for one last time.

He was lying there unconscious, just like the first time she had seen him. Even now she still felt a strong physical attraction to him, but Karishma knew she would be fine. She was fine after Varun. She was fine even after breaking up with her first high school sweetheart, Anil, although his car accident was only partially her fault.

"Ok, it was totally my fault" Karishma smiled remembering cutting the brake lines. "Cars are like people, you can break them so easily," she giggled at her own joke. "Maybe it's time to give a chance to that handsome German doctor Franz. Karishma and Franz Wolfrathausen sounds not too shabby," she thought while putting on a blonde wig and oversized glasses that covered her face. She gave one last nod to Rakesh. The only thing Karishma regretted was not having one last farewell sex.

TO BE CONTINUED ...

Printed in Great Britain
by Amazon